Who Killed Zebedee?

and

John Jago's Ghost

Wilkie Collins

ET REMOTISSIMA PROPE

100 PAGES

100 PAGES
Published by Hesperus Press Limited
4 Rickett Street, London SW6 1RU
www.hesperuspress.com

'Who Killed Zebedee?' first published 1881
'John Jago's Ghost' first published 1873–4
First published by Hesperus Press Limited, 2002

Foreword © Martin Jarvis, 2002

Designed and typeset by Fraser Muggeridge
Printed in the United Arab Emirates by Oriental Press

ISBN: 1-84391-019-5

CONTENTS

FOREWORD

'Who Killed Zebedee?' first appeared in January 1881 in a publication breezily entitled *The Seaside Library*. It begins with a cryptic deathbed prologue, before Collins suddenly leaps back in time and jolts us to frantic attention at the dramatic entrance of an attractive young woman into a police station. It's as visual as any film. Try this for a trailer:

Priscilla (played by Kate Winslet of course): 'Murder's the matter! For God's sake come back with me... A young woman has murdered her husband in the night! With a knife, sir. She says she thinks she did it in her sleep... Oh, why did I ever set foot in that horrible house?'

Aha! Cut to reaction-shot of sympathetic young constable. (Jude Law please.) Dissolve to interior bedroom. Pan across body of victim. Zoom into close-up on knife. Psycho-style screaming strings. Gravelly voice-over: 'Who Killed Zebedee? In your wildest nightmares you'd never guess the truth. It's *murder* – coming soon to a cinema near you...!'

Every detective story we have ever seen, read or heard owes a debt to Wilkie Collins. 'Who Killed Zebedee?' is the short-form work of a master of the genre. Genre? Some would argue he even invented it. In his great novel of detection *The Moonstone,* published thirteen years earlier, the stringy Sergeant Cuff was already investigating the midnight mysteries of somnambulism. But don't be fooled. There's something quite different going on here: an ambitious young officer needs to solve a deadly conundrum to secure promotion and, as a bonus, win the girl who assists him.

Whodunit? Was it really the wife? The butler? I'm not telling, since I want you to enjoy the same frisson I experienced in delving into this box of literary tricks. Like a movie of the mind, Collins' hand-held narrative lens probes all the nooks and crannies of Mrs Crosscapel's lodging-house. His delineation of character, too, is consummate. Agatha Christie, writing forty and more years later, learned how to pluck unexpected rabbits out of surprising hats, but was never able to beget the same kind of flesh – and blood. Collins invariably provides us with believable people, trustworthy or not. In 'Zebedee' there's a formidable list of suspects, any one of whom might have wielded the fatal instrument. Mr Deluc perhaps, skulking on the stairs, ready for his close-up? First choice for the role is Jim Broadbent, waving a cigar and pleading, 'It isn't insensibility to this terrible tragedy… My nerves have been shattered, Mr Policeman, and I can only repair the mischief in this way…'

Could the culprit be respectable little Miss Mybus (check Judi Dench's availability) who lodges in the back parlour? 'The policeman can come in,' she calls out, 'if he will promise not to look at me.' Does her Mrs Micawber manner hide a darker purpose? And what is that smell emanating from the landlady's kitchen? Do we detect the salty aroma of an early fictional red herring? Despite being posed these entertaining riddles, the reader – as with *The Moonstone* and the atmospheric *Woman in White* (1860) – never for a moment feels that the dramatis personae are purely serving a crossword-puzzle plot. I suspect Colin Dexter would be more than happy to have penned this ironic human exchange on the subject of police procedure: 'You know the form if any statement is volunteered?'

'Yes, sir. I am to caution the persons that whatever they say will be taken down, and may be used against them.'

'Quite right. You'll be an inspector yourself one of these days.'

Collins, donating a scene for Inspector Morse and Sergeant Lewis a century in advance.

'John Jago's Ghost' is a longer work and was much enjoyed as a serial in *The Home Journal* from December 1873 to February 1874. It, too, opens with a teaser, but this time our hero Philip Lefranc (a barrister like his creator) is told by his doctor that he is not to die. He is merely to travel for the good of his health to, as it turns out, an Old Dark House. Collins is blazing a trail that Bram Stoker, Conan Doyle, Dorothy L. Sayers, Daphne du Maurier, even P.D. James and Stephen King were to follow. Dickens had died the year before and we may perceive, among the shadows, the ghost of Miss Haversham, and catch the cries of old Orlick breathing his last in the limekiln out on the marshes. Well, what's a nuance or two among such collaborative friends as Charles and Wilkie? They had worked together on many theatrical and literary projects between 1855 and 1867, notably the journals *Household Words* and *All The Year Round*. Lefranc's spooky excursion to America is even more alarming than young Chuzzlewit's trip of thirty years before.

Philip arrives at Morwick Farm. 'There was no forewarning, in the appearance of Ambrose Meadowcroft, of the strange and terrible events that were to follow my arrival...' (Step forward Brad Pitt.) But soon Philip finds a graver stateside version of the cold comfort that Stella Gibbons had fun with sixty years later, and encounters a further cast of players led, I fancy, by Jack Nicholson as the enigmatic estate-worker John Jago. And will Gwyneth Paltrow be available for winsome Naomi Colebrook? There's a page-turning sense of foreboding in Collins' account of the rivalry between amiable Ambrose and his saturnine brother Silas (thank you Tom

Cruise) in their shared suspicion of Jago. Mysterious conversations at dead of night, moonlight meetings, mischief, romance – it's all here. But what's going to happen? To whom? Listen to Naomi whispering her fears to Philip: 'John gives the orders now. The boys do the work; but they have no voice in it when John and the old man put their heads together... If Silas had not caught the knife in his hand... it might have ended, for anything I know, in murder –' Ooh-er. And when do we get to see the ghost? You bet there's enough shenanigans afoot down on this farm to tax the combined brain-cells of Cuff, Sherlock and Hercule, not to mention Miss Marple. Naturally it's left to our convalescing Brit to do his darnedest. (By the way, has Hugh Grant accepted yet?)

So what *is* that nasty something lurking within the Morwick woodsheds? Shall I disclose its deathly secret? It's – but no, better to keep quiet, your Honour, before I'm arrested for 'squealing' and end up in that worrying limekiln – still squealing no doubt.

To sum up, members of the jury, here is a last exhibit from this gripping chiller:

'Remember that what he said might be taken down in writing...'

Indeed, Inspector. Wilkie Collins' writing has been taken down and used, not against him, but as a sensational tribute over the years. A continuing testimony to his techniques of detective, mystery and murder fiction, still enjoyed by us today.

I rest my case.

– *Martin Jarvis, 2002*

Who Killed Zebedee?

Before the doctor left me one evening, I asked him how much longer I was likely to live. He answered, 'It's not easy to say; you may die before I can get back to you in the morning, or you may live to the end of the month.'

I was alive enough on the next morning to think of the needs of my soul, and (being a member of the Roman Catholic Church) to send for a priest.

The history of my sins, related in confession, included blameworthy neglect of a duty which I owed to the laws of my country. In the priest's opinion – and I agreed with him – I was bound to make public acknowledgement of my fault, as an act of penance becoming to a Catholic Englishman. We concluded, thereupon, to try a division of labour. I related the circumstances, while his reverence took the pen, and put the matter into shape.

Here follows what came of it.

When I was a young man of five and twenty, I became a member of the London police force. After nearly two years' ordinary experience of the responsible and ill-paid duties of that vocation, I found myself employed on my first serious and terrible case of official enquiry – relating to nothing less than the crime of murder.

The circumstances were these.

I was then attached to a station in the northern district of London – which I beg permission not to mention more particularly. On a certain Monday in the week, I took my turn of night duty. Up to four in the morning, nothing occurred at the station house out of the ordinary way. It was then springtime, and, between the gas and the fire, the room became rather hot. I went to the door to get a breath of fresh air – much to the surprise of our inspector on duty, who was constitutionally a chilly man. There was a fine rain falling, and a nasty damp in the air sent me back to the fireside. I don't suppose I had sat down for more than a minute when the swinging door was violently pushed open. A frantic woman ran in with a scream, and said, 'Is this the station house?'

Our inspector (otherwise an excellent officer) had, by some perversity of nature, a hot temper in his chilly constitution. 'Why, bless the woman, can't you *see* it is?' he says. 'What's the matter now?'

'Murder's the matter!' she burst out. 'For God's sake come back with me. It's at Mrs Crosscapel's lodging-house, number fourteen, Lehigh Street. A young woman has murdered her husband in the night! With a knife, sir. She says she thinks she did it in her sleep.'

I confess I was startled by this; and the third man on duty (a sergeant) seemed to feel it too. She was a nice-looking young woman, even in her terrified condition, just out of bed, with her clothes huddled on her anyhow. I was partial in those days to a tall figure – and she was, as they say, my style. I put a chair for her; and the sergeant poked the fire. As for the inspector, nothing ever upset *him*. He questioned her as coolly as if it had been a case of petty larceny.

'Have you seen the murdered man?' he asked.

'No, sir.'

'Or the wife?'

'No, sir. I didn't dare go into the room. I only heard about it!'

'Oh? And who are you? One of the lodgers?'

'No, sir. I'm the cook.'

'Isn't there a master in the house?'

'Yes, sir. He's frightened out of his wits. And the house-maid's gone for the doctor. It all falls on the poor servants, of course. Oh, why did I ever set foot in that horrible house?'

The poor soul burst out crying, and shivered from head to foot. The inspector made a note of her statement, and then asked her to read it, and sign it with her name. The object of this proceeding was to get her to come near enough to give him the opportunity of smelling her breath. 'When people make extraordinary statements,' he afterwards said to me, 'it sometimes saves trouble to satisfy yourself that they are not drunk. I've known them to be mad – but not often. You will generally find *that* in their eyes.'

She roused herself and signed her name – Priscilla Thurlby. The inspector's own test proved her to be sober; and her eyes – of a nice light-blue colour, mild and pleasant, no doubt, when they were not staring with fear, and red with crying – satisfied him (as I supposed) that she was not mad. He turned the case over to me in the first instance. I saw that he didn't believe in it, even yet.

'Go back with her to the house,' he says. 'This may be a stupid hoax, or a quarrel exaggerated. See to it yourself, and hear what the doctor says. If it *is* serious, send word back here directly, and let nobody enter the place or leave it till we come. Stop! You know the form if any statement is volunteered?'

'Yes, sir. I am to caution the persons that whatever they say will be taken down, and may be used against them.'

'Quite right. You'll be an inspector yourself one of these days. Now, miss!' With that, he dismissed her, under my care.

Lehigh Street was not very far off – about twenty minutes' walk from the station. I confess I thought the inspector had been rather hard on Priscilla. She was herself naturally angry with him. 'What does he mean?', she says, 'by talking of a hoax? I wish he was as frightened as I am. This is the first time I have been out at service, sir – and I did think I had found a respectable place.'

I said very little to her – feeling, if the truth must be told, rather anxious about the duty committed to me. On reaching the house the door was opened from within, before I could knock. A gentleman stepped out, who proved to be the doctor. He stopped the moment he saw me.

'You must be careful, policeman,' he says. 'I found the man lying on his back, in bed, dead – with the knife that had killed him left sticking in the wound.'

Hearing this, I felt the necessity of sending at once to the station. Where could I find a trustworthy messenger? I took the liberty of asking the doctor if he would repeat to the police what he had already said to me. The station was not much out of his way home. He kindly granted my request.

The landlady (Mrs Crosscapel) joined us while we were talking. She was still a young woman; not easily frightened, as far as I can see, even by a murder in the house. Her husband was in the passage behind her. He looked old enough to be her father; and he so trembled with terror that some people might have taken him for the guilty person. I removed the key from the street door, after locking it. Then I said to the landlady, 'Nobody must leave the house, or enter the house, till the inspector comes. I must examine the premises to see if anyone has broken in.'

'There is the key of the area gate,' she said, in answer to me. 'It's always kept locked. Come downstairs and see for yourself.' Priscilla went with us. Her mistress set her to work to light the kitchen fire. 'Some of us,' says Mrs Crosscapel, 'may be better for a cup of tea.' I remarked that she took things easy, under the circumstances. She answered that the landlady of a lodging-house could not afford to lose her wits, no matter what might happen.

I found the gate locked, and the shutters of the kitchen window fastened. The back kitchen and back door were secured in the same way. No person was concealed anywhere. Returning upstairs, I examined the front parlour window. There again, the barred shutters answered for the security of that room. A cracked voice spoke through the door of the back parlour. 'The policeman can come in,' it said, 'if he will promise not to look at me.' I turned to the landlady for information. 'It's my parlour lodger, Miss Mybus,' she said, 'a most respectable lady.' Going into the room, I saw something rolled up perpendicularly in the bed curtains. Miss Mybus had made herself modestly invisible in that way. Having now satisfied my mind about the security of the lower part of the house, and having the keys safe in my pocket, I was ready to go upstairs.

On our way to the upper regions, I asked if there had been any visitors on the previous day. There had been only two

8

visitors, friends of the lodgers – and Mrs Crosscapel herself had let them both out. My next enquiry related to the lodgers themselves. On the ground floor there was Miss Mybus. On the first floor (occupying both rooms) Mr Barfield, an old bachelor, employed in a merchant's office. On the second floor, in the front room, Mr John Zebedee, the murdered man, and his wife. In the back room, Mr Deluc, described as a cigar-agent, and supposed to be a Creole gentleman from Martinique. In the front garret, Mr and Mrs Crosscapel. In the back garret, the cook and the housemaid. These were the inhabitants, regularly accounted for. I asked about the servants. 'Both excellent characters,' says the landlady, 'or they would not be in my service.'

We reached the second floor, and found the housemaid on the watch outside the door of the front room. Not as nice a woman, personally, as the cook, and sadly frightened of course. Her mistress had posted her, to give the alarm in the case of an outbreak on the part of Mrs Zebedee, kept locked up in her room. My arrival relieved the housemaid of further responsibility. She ran downstairs to her fellow-servant in the kitchen.

I asked Mrs Crosscapel how and when the alarm of the murder had been given.

'Soon after three this morning,' says she, 'I was woke here by the screams of Mrs Zebedee. I found her out here on the landing, and Mr Deluc, in great alarm, trying to quiet her. Sleeping in the next room, he had only to open his door, when her screams woke him. "My dear John's murdered! I am the miserable wretch – I did it in my sleep!" She repeated those frantic words over and over again, until she dropped in a swoon. Mr Deluc and I carried her back into the bedroom. We both thought the poor creature had been driven distracted by some dreadful dream. But when we got to the bedside – don't ask me what we saw, the doctor has told you about it already. I was once a nurse in a hospital, and accustomed, as such, to horrid sights. It turned me cold and giddy, notwithstanding. As for Mr Deluc, I thought *he* would have a fainting fit next.'

Hearing this, I enquired if Mrs Zebedee had said or done any strange things since she had been Mrs Crosscapel's lodger.

'You think she's mad?' says the landlady. 'And anybody would be of your mind, when a woman accuses herself of murdering her husband in her sleep. All I can say is that, up to this morning, a more quiet, sensible, well-behaved little person than Mrs Zebedee I never met with. Only just married, mind, and as fond of her unfortunate husband as a woman could be. I should have called them a pattern couple, in their own line of life.'

There was no more to be said on the landing. We unlocked the door and went into the room.

2

He lay in his bed on his back as the doctor had described him. On the left side of his nightgown, just over his heart, the blood on the linen told its terrible tale. As well as one could judge, looking unwillingly at a dead face, he must have been a handsome young man in his lifetime. It was a sight to sadden anybody – but I think the most painful sensation was when my eyes fell next on his miserable wife.

She was down on the floor, crouched up in a corner – a dark little woman, smartly dressed in gay colours. Her black hair and her big brown eyes made the horrid paleness of her face look even more deadly white than perhaps it really was. She stared straight at us without appearing to see us. We spoke to her, and she never answered a word. She might have been dead – like her husband – except that she perpetually picked at her fingers, and shuddered every now and then as if she was cold. I went to her and tried to lift her up. She shrank back with a cry that well-nigh frightened me – not because it was loud, but because it was more like the cry of some animal than of a human being. However quietly she might have behaved in the landlady's previous experience of her, she was beside herself now. I might have been moved by a natural pity for her, or I might have been completely upset in my mind – I only know this: I could not persuade myself that she was guilty. I even said to Mrs Crosscapel, 'I don't believe she did it.'

While I spoke, there was a knock at the door. I went downstairs at once, and admitted (to my great relief) the inspector, accompanied by one of our men.

He waited downstairs to hear my report, and he approved of what I had done. 'It looks as if the murder had been committed by somebody in the house.' Saying this, he left the man below, and went up with me to the second floor.

Before he had been a minute in the room, he discovered an object which had escaped my observation.

It was the knife that had done the deed.

The doctor had found it left in the body, had withdrawn it to probe the wound, and had laid it on the bedside-table. It was one of those useful knives which contain a saw, a corkscrew, and other like implements. The big blade fastened back, when open, with a spring. Except where there was blood on it, it was as bright as when it had been purchased. A small metal plate was fastened to the horn handle, containing an inscription, only partly engraved, which ran thus: 'To John Zebedee, from – '. There it stopped, strangely enough.

Who or what had interrupted the engraver's work? It was

impossible even to guess. Nevertheless, the inspector was encouraged.

'This ought to help us,' he said – and then he gave an attentive ear (looking all the while at the poor creature in the corner) to what Mrs Crosscapel had to tell him.

The landlady having done, he said he must now see the lodger who slept in the next bedchamber.

Mr Deluc made his appearance, standing at the door of the room, and turning away his head in horror from the sight inside.

He was wrapped in a splendid blue dressing-gown, with a golden girdle and trimmings. His scanty brownish hair curled (whether artificially or not, I am unable to say) in little ringlets. His complexion was yellow. His greenish-brown eyes were of the sort called 'goggle' – they looked as if they might drop out of his face if you held a spoon under them. His moustache and goat's beard were beautifully oiled, and, to complete his equipment, he had a long black cigar in his mouth.

'It isn't insensibility to this terrible tragedy,' he explained. 'My nerves have been shattered, Mr Policeman, and I can only repair the mischief in this way. Be pleased to excuse and feel for me.'

The inspector questioned this witness sharply and closely. He was not a man to be misled by appearances, but I could see that he was far from liking, or even trusting, Mr Deluc. Nothing came of the examination, except what Mrs Crosscapel had in substance already mentioned to me. Mr Deluc returned to his room.

'How long has he been lodging with you?' the inspector asked, as soon as his back was turned.

'Nearly a year,' the landlady answered.

'Did he give a reference?'

'As good a reference as I could wish for.' Thereupon, she mentioned the names of a well-known firm of cigar merchants in the City. The inspector noted the information in his pocketbook.

I would rather not relate in detail what happened next: it is too distressing to be dwelt on. Let me only say that the poor demented woman was taken away in a cab to the station house. The inspector possessed himself of the knife, and of a book found on the floor, called *The World of Sleep*. The portmanteau containing the luggage was locked – and then the door of the room was secured, the keys in both cases being left in my charge. My instructions were to remain in the house, and allow nobody to leave it, until I heard again shortly from the inspector.

3

The coroner's inquest was adjourned and the examination before the magistrate ended in a remand – Mrs Zebedee being in no condition to understand the proceedings in either case. The surgeon reported her to be completely prostrated by a terrible nervous shock. When he was asked if he considered her to have been a sane woman before the murder took place, he refused to answer positively at that time.

A week passed. The murdered man was buried, his old father attending the funeral. I occasionally saw Mrs Crosscapel, and the two servants, for the purpose of getting such further information as was thought desirable. Both the cook and the housemaid had given their month's notice to quit – declining, in the interest of their characters, to remain in a house which had been the scene of a murder. Mr Deluc's nerves led also to his removal; his rest was now disturbed by frightful dreams. He paid the necessary forfeit-money, and left without notice. The first-floor lodger, Mr Barfield, kept his rooms, but obtained leave of absence from his employers, and took refuge with some friends in the country. Miss Mybus alone remained in the parlours. 'When I am comfortable,' the old lady said, 'nothing moves me, at my age. A murder up two pairs of stairs is nearly the same thing as a murder in the next house. Distance, you see, makes all the difference.'

It mattered little to the police what the lodgers did. We had men in plain clothes watching the house night and day. Everybody who went away was privately followed, and the police in the district kept an eye on them, after that. As long as we failed to put Mrs Zebedee's extraordinary statement to any sort of test – to say nothing of having proved unsuccessful, thus far, in tracing the knife to its purchaser – we were bound to let no person living under Mrs Crosscapel's roof, on the night of the murder, slip through our fingers.

4

In a fortnight more, Mrs Zebedee had sufficiently recovered to make the necessary statement – after the preliminary caution addressed to persons in such cases. The surgeon had no hesitation now in reporting her to be a sane woman.

Her station in life had been domestic service. She had lived for four years in her last place as lady's maid, with a family residing in Dorsetshire. The one objection to her had been the occasional infirmity of sleepwalking, which made it necessary that one of the other female servants should sleep in the same room, with the door locked and the key under her pillow. In all other respects the lady's maid was described by her mistress as 'a perfect treasure'.

In the last six months of her service, a young man named John Zebedee entered the house (with a written character) as footman. He soon fell in love with the nice little lady's maid, and she heartily returned the feeling. They might have waited for years before they were in a pecuniary position to marry, but for the death of Zebedee's uncle, who left him a little fortune of two thousand pounds. They were now, for persons in their station, rich enough to please themselves, and they were married from the house in which they had served together, the little daughters of the family showing their affection for Mrs Zebedee by acting as her bridesmaids.

The young husband was a careful man. He decided to employ his small capital to the best advantage, by sheep-farming in Australia. His wife made no objection. She was ready to go wherever John went.

Accordingly they spent their short honeymoon in London, so as to see for themselves the vessel in which their passage was to be taken. They went to Mrs Crosscapel's lodging-house because Zebedee's uncle had always stayed there in London. Ten days were to pass before the day of embarkation arrived. This gave the young couple a welcome holiday, and a prospect of amusing themselves to their hearts' content among the sights and shows of the great city.

On their first evening in London they went to the theatre. They were both accustomed to the fresh air of the country, and they felt half stifled by the heat and the gas. However, they were so pleased with an amusement which was new to them that they went to another theatre on the next evening. On this second occasion, John Zebedee found the heat unendurable. They left the theatre, and got back to their lodgings towards ten o'clock.

Let the rest be told in the words used by Mrs Zebedee herself. She said:

'We sat talking for a little while in our room, and John's

headache got worse and worse. I persuaded him to go to bed, and I put out the candle (the fire giving sufficient light to undress by), so that he might the sooner fall asleep. But he was too restless to sleep. He asked me to read him something. Books always made him drowsy at the best of times.

'I had not myself begun to undress. So I lit the candle again, and I opened the only book I had. John had noticed it at the railway bookstall by the name of *The World of Sleep*. He used to joke with me about my being a sleepwalker, and he said, "Here's something that's sure to interest you" – and he made me a present of the book.

'Before I had read to him for more than half an hour he was fast asleep. Not feeling that way inclined, I went on reading to myself.

'The book did indeed interest me. There was one terrible story which took a hold on my mind – the story of a man who stabbed his own wife in a sleepwalking dream. I thought of putting down my book after that, and then changed my mind again and went on. The next chapters were not so interesting. They were full of learned accounts of why we fall asleep, and what our brains do in that state, and such like. It ended in my falling asleep, too, in my armchair by the fireside.

'I don't know what o'clock it was when I went to sleep. I don't know how long I slept, or whether I dreamed or not. The candle and the fire had both burned out, and it was pitch dark when I woke. I can't even say why I woke – unless it was the coldness of the room.

'There was a spare candle on the chimney-piece. I found the matchbox, and got a light. Then, for the first time, I turned round towards the bed; and I saw –'

She had seen the dead body of her husband, murdered while she was unconsciously at his side – and she fainted, poor creature, at the bare remembrance of it.

The proceedings were adjourned. She received every possible care and attention, the chaplain looking after her welfare as well as the surgeon.

I have said nothing of the evidence of the landlady and the servants. It was taken as a mere formality. What little they knew proved nothing against Mrs Zebedee. The police made no discoveries that supported her first frantic accusation of herself. Her master and mistress, where she had been last in service, spoke of her in the highest terms. We were at a complete deadlock.

It had been thought best not to surprise Mr Deluc, as yet, by citing him as a witness. The action of the law was, however, hurried in this case by a private communication received from the chaplain.

After twice seeing and speaking with Mrs Zebedee, the reverend gentleman was persuaded that she had no more to do than himself with the murder of her husband. He did not consider that he was justified in repeating a confidential communication – he would only recommend that Mr Deluc should be summoned to appear at the next examination. This advice was followed.

The police had no evidence against Mrs Zebedee when the enquiry was resumed. To assist the ends of justice she was now put into the witness-box. The discovery of her murdered husband when she woke in the small hours of the morning was passed over as rapidly as possible. Only three questions of importance were put to her.

First, the knife was produced. Had she ever seen it in her husband's possession? Never. Did she know anything about it? Nothing whatever.

Secondly, did she, or did her husband, lock the bedroom

door when they returned from the theatre? No. Did she afterwards lock the door herself? No.

Thirdly, had she any sort of reason to give for supposing that she had murdered her husband in a sleepwalking dream? No reason, except that she was beside herself at the time, and the book put the thought into her head.

After this the other witnesses were sent out of court. The motive for the chaplain's communication now appeared.

Mrs Zebedee was asked if anything unpleasant had occurred between Mr Deluc and herself.

Yes. He had caught her alone on the stairs at the lodging-house, had presumed to make love to her, and had carried the insult still further by attempting to kiss her. She had slapped his face, and had declared that her husband should know of it if his misconduct was repeated. He was in a furious rage at having his face slapped, and he said to her, 'Madam, you may live to regret this.'

After consultation, and at the request of our inspector, it was decided to keep Mr Deluc in ignorance of Mrs Zebedee's statement for the present. When the witnesses were recalled, he gave the same evidence which he had already given to the inspector – and he was then asked if he knew anything of the knife. He looked at it without any guilty signs in his face, and swore that he had never seen it before that moment. The resumed enquiry ended, and still nothing had been discovered.

But we kept an eye on Mr Deluc. Our next effort was to try if we could associate him with the purchase of the knife.

Here again (there really did seem to be a sort of fatality in this case) we reached no useful result. It was easy enough to find out the wholesale cutlers, who had manufactured the knife at Sheffield, by the mark on the blade. But they made tens of thousands of such knives, and disposed of them to foreign parts. As to finding out the person who had engraved the imperfect inscription (without knowing where, or by whom, the knife had been purchased) we might as well have looked for the proverbial needle in the bundle of hay. Our last resource was to have the knife photographed, with the inscribed side uppermost, and to send copies to every police station in the kingdom.

At the same time we reckoned up Mr Deluc – I mean that we made investigations into his past life – on the chance that he and the murdered man might have known each other, and might have had a quarrel, or a rivalry about a woman, on some former occasion. No such discovery rewarded us.

We found Deluc to have led a dissipated life, and to have mixed with very bad company. But he had kept out of reach of the law. A man may be a profligate vagabond, may insult a lady, may say threatening things to her in the first stinging sensation of having his face slapped – but it doesn't follow from these blots on his character that he has murdered her husband in the dead of the night.

Once more, then, when we were called upon to report ourselves, we had no evidence to produce. The photographs failed to discover the owner of the knife, and to explain its interrupted inscription. Poor Mrs Zebedee was allowed to go back to her friends, on entering into her own recognisance to appear again if called upon. Articles in the newspapers began to enquire how many more murderers would succeed in baffling the police. The authorities at the Treasury offered a reward of a hundred pounds for the necessary information. And the weeks passed, and nobody claimed the reward.

Our inspector was not a man to be easily beaten. More enquiries and examinations followed. It is needless to say anything about them. We were defeated – and there, so far as the police and the public were concerned, was an end of it. The assassination of the poor young husband soon passed out of notice, like other undiscovered murders. One obscure person only was foolish enough, in his leisure hours, to persist in trying to solve the problem of who killed Zebedee. He felt that he might rise to the highest position in the police force if he succeeded where his elders and betters had failed – and he held to his own little ambition, though everybody laughed at him. In plain English, I was the man.

5

Without meaning it, I have told my story ungratefully.

There were two persons who saw nothing in my resolution to continue the investigation single-handed. One of them was Miss Mybus, and the other was the cook, Priscilla Thurlby.

Mentioning the lady first, Miss Mybus was indignant at the resigned manner in which the police accepted their defeat. She was a little bright-eyed wiry woman, and she spoke her mind freely.

'This comes home to me,' she said. 'Just look back for a year or two. I can call to mind two cases of persons found murdered in London – and the assassins have never been traced. I am a person too, and I asked myself if my turn is not coming next. You're a nice-looking fellow – and I like your pluck and perseverance. Come here as often as you think right; and say you are my visitor if they make any difficulty about letting you in. One thing more! I have nothing particular to do, and I am no fool. Here, in the parlours, I see everybody who comes into the house or goes out of the house. Leave me your address – I may get some information for you yet.'

With the best intentions, Miss Mybus found no opportunity

of helping me. Of the two, Priscilla Thurlby seemed more likely to be of use.

In the first place, she was sharp and active, and (not having succeeded in getting another situation as yet) was mistress of her own movements.

In the second place, she was a woman I could trust. Before she left home to try domestic service in London, the parson of her native parish gave her a written testimonial, of which I append a copy. Thus it ran:

> *I gladly recommend Priscilla Thurlby for any respectable employment which she may be competent to undertake. Her father and mother are infirm old people, who have lately suffered a diminution of their income; and they have a younger daughter to maintain. Rather than be a burden on her parents, Priscilla goes to London to find domestic employment, and to devote her earnings to the assistance of her father and mother. This circumstance speaks for itself. I have known the family many years, and I only regret that I have no vacant place in my own household which I can offer to this good girl.*
>
> *(Signed)*
> *Henry Derrington, Rector of Roth.*

After reading those words, I could safely ask Priscilla to help me in reopening the mysterious murder case to some good purpose.

My notion was that the proceedings of the persons in Mrs Crosscapel's house had not been closely enough enquired into yet. By way of continuing the investigation, I asked Priscilla if she could tell me anything which associated the housemaid with Mr Deluc. She was unwilling to answer. 'I may be casting suspicion on an innocent person,' she said. 'Besides, I was for so short a time the housemaid's fellow-servant –'

'You slept in the same room with her,' I remarked, 'and you had opportunities of observing her conduct towards the lodgers. If they had asked you, at the examination, what I now ask, you would have answered as an honest woman.'

To this argument she yielded. I heard from her particulars which threw a new light on Mr Deluc, and on the case generally. On that information I acted. It was slow work, owing to the claims on me of my regular duties, but with Priscilla's help, I steadily advanced towards the end I had in view.

Besides this, I owed another obligation to Mrs Crosscapel's nice-looking cook. The confession must be made sooner or later – and I may as well make it now. I first knew what love was, thanks to Priscilla. I had delicious kisses, thanks to Priscilla. And, when I asked if she would marry me, she didn't say no. She looked, I must own, a little sadly, and she said, 'How can two such poor people as we are ever hope to marry?' To this I answered, 'It won't be long before I lay my hand on the clue which my inspector has failed to find. I shall be in a position to marry you, my dear, when the time comes.'

At our next meeting we spoke of her parents. I was now her promised husband. Judging by what I had heard of the proceedings of other people in my position, it seemed to be only right that I should be made known to her father and mother. She entirely agreed with me, and she wrote home that day, to tell them to expect us at the end of the week.

I took my turn of night duty, and so gained my liberty for the greater part of the next day. I dressed myself in plain clothes, and we took our tickets on the railway for Yateland, being the nearest station to the village in which Priscilla's parents lived.

6

The train stopped, as usual, at the big town of Waterbank. Supporting herself by her needle, while she was still unprovided with a situation, Priscilla had been at work late in the night – she was tired and thirsty. I left the carriage to get some soda-water. The stupid girl in the refreshment room failed to pull the cork out of the bottle, and refused to let me help her. She took a corkscrew, and used it crookedly. I lost all patience, and snatched the bottle out of her hand. Just as I drew the cork, the bell rang on the platform. I only waited to pour the soda-water into a glass – but the train was moving as I left the refreshment-room. The porters stopped me when I tried to jump onto the step of the carriage. I was left behind.

As soon as I had recovered my temper, I looked at the timetable. We had reached Waterbank at five minutes past one, and arrived at Yateland (the next station) ten minutes afterwards. I could only hope that Priscilla would look at the timetable too, and wait for me. If I had attempted to walk the distance between the two places, I should have lost time instead of saving it. The interval before me was not very long; I occupied it in looking over the town.

Speaking with all due respect to the inhabitants, Waterbank (to other people) is a dull place. I went up one street and down another – and stopped to look at a shop which struck me; not from anything in itself, but because it was the only shop in the street with the shutters closed.

A bill was posted on the shutters, announcing that the place was to let. The out-going tradesman's name and business, announced in the customary painted letters, ran thus: *James Wycomb, Cutler etc.*

For the first time, it occurred to me that we had forgotten an obstacle in our way when we distributed our photographs of the knife. We had none of us remembered that a certain portion of cutlers might be placed, by circumstances, out of our reach – either by retiring from business or becoming bankrupt. I always carried a copy of the photograph about me, and I thought to myself, 'Here is the ghost of a chance of tracing the knife to Mr Deluc!'

The shop door was opened, after I had twice rung the bell, by an old man, very dirty and very deaf. He said, 'You had better go upstairs, and speak to Mr Scorrier – top of the house.'

I put my lips to the old fellow's ear-trumpet, and asked who Mr Scorrier was.

'Brother-in-law to Mr Wycomb. Mr Wycomb's dead. If you want to buy the business apply to Mr Scorrier.'

Receiving that reply, I went upstairs, and found Mr Scorrier engaged in engraving a brass door-plate. He was a middle-aged man, with a cadaverous face and dim eyes. After the necessary apologies, I produced my photograph.

'May I ask, sir, if you know anything of the inscription on that knife?' I said.

He took his magnifying glass to look at it.

'This is curious,' he remarked quietly. 'I remember the queer name – Zebedee. Yes, sir, I did the engraving, as far as it goes. I wonder what prevented me from finishing it?'

The name of Zebedee, and the unfinished inscription on the knife, had appeared in every English newspaper. He took the matter so coolly that I was doubtful how to interpret his answer. Was it possible that he had not seen the account of the murder? Or was he an accomplice with prodigious powers of self-control?

'Excuse me,' I said, 'do you read the newspapers?'

'Never! My eyesight is failing me. I abstain from reading in the interests of my occupation.'

'Have you not heard the name of Zebedee mentioned – particularly by people who do read the newspapers?'

'Very likely, but I didn't attend it. When the day's work is done, I take my walk. Then I have my supper, my drop of grog, and my pipe. Then I go to bed. A dull existence you think, I dare say! I had a miserable life, sir, when I was young. A bare subsistence, and a little rest, before the last perfect rest in the grave – that is all I want. The world has gone by me long ago. So much the better.'

The poor man spoke honestly. I was ashamed of having doubted him. I returned to the subject of the knife.

'Do you know where it was purchased, and by whom?' I asked.

'My memory is not so good as it was,' he said, 'but I have something by me that helps it.'

He took from a cupboard a dirty old scrapbook. Strips of paper, with writing on them, were pasted on the pages, as well as I could see. He turned to an index, or table of contents, and opened a page. Something like a flash of life showed on his dismal face.

'Ha! now I remember,' he said. 'The knife was bought of my late brother-in-law, in the shop downstairs. It all comes back to me, sir. A person in a state of frenzy burst into this very room, and snatched the knife away from me, when I was only halfway through the inscription!'

I felt that I was now close on discovery. 'May I see what it is that has assisted your memory?' I asked.

'Oh yes. You must know, sir, I live by engraving inscriptions and addresses, and I paste in this book the manuscript inscriptions which I receive, with marks of my own on the margin. For one thing, they serve as a reference to new customers. And for another thing, they do certainly help my memory.'

He turned the book towards me, and pointed to a slip of paper which occupied the lower half of a page.

I read the complete inscription, intended for the knife that killed Zebedee, and written as follows:

'To John Zebedee. From Priscilla Thurlby.'

7

I declare that it is impossible for me to describe what I felt when Priscilla's name confronted me like a written confession of guilt. How long it was before I recovered myself in some degree, I cannot say. The only thing I can clearly call to mind is that I frightened the poor engraver.

My first desire was to get possession of the manuscript inscription. I told him I was a policeman, and summoned him to assist me in the discovery of a crime. I even offered him money. He drew back from my hand. 'You shall have it for nothing,' he said, 'if you will only go away and never come back here again.' He tried to cut it out of the page – but his trembling hands were helpless. I cut it out myself, and attempted to thank him. He wouldn't hear me. 'Go away!' he said, 'I don't like the look of you.'

It may be here objected that I ought not to have felt so sure as I did of the woman's guilt, until I had got more evidence against her. The knife might have been stolen from her, supposing she was the person who had snatched it out of the engraver's hands, and might have been afterwards used by the thief to commit the murder. All very true. But I never had a moment's doubt in my own mind from the time when I read the damnable line in the engraver's book.

I went back to the railway without any plan in my head. The train by which I had proposed to follow her had left Water-bank. The next train that arrived was for London. I took my place in it – still without any plan in my head.

At Charing Cross a friend met me. He said, 'You're looking miserably ill. Come and have a drink.'

I went with him. The liquor was what I really wanted. It strung me up, and cleared my head. He went his way, and I went mine. In a little while more, I determined what I would do.

In the first place, I decided to resign my situation in the police, from a motive which will presently appear. In the second place, I took a bed at a public house. She would no doubt return to London, and she would go to my lodgings to find out why I had broken my appointment. To bring to justice the one woman whom I had dearly loved was too cruel a duty for a poor creature like me. I preferred leaving the police force. On the other hand, if she and I met before time had helped me to control myself, I had a horrid fear that I might turn murderer next, and kill her then and there. The wretch had not only all but misled me into marrying her, but also into charging the innocent housemaid with being concerned in the murder.

The same night I hit on a way of clearing up such doubts as still harassed my mind. I wrote to the rector of Roth, informing him that I was engaged to marry her, and asking if he would tell me (in consideration of my position) what her former relations might have been with the person named John Zebedee.

By return of post I got this reply:

Sir, under the circumstances, I think I am bound to tell you confidentially what the friends and well-wishers of Priscilla have kept secret, for her sake.

Zebedee was in service in this neighbourhood. I am sorry to say it, of a man who has come to such a miserable end – but his behaviour to Priscilla proves him to have

*been a vicious and heartless wretch. They were engaged –
and, I add with indignation, he tried to seduce her under a
promise of marriage. Her virtue resisted him, and he
pretended to be ashamed of himself. The banns were
published in my church. On the next day Zebedee
disappeared, and cruelly deserted her. He was a capable
servant, and I believe he got another place. I leave you to
imagine what the poor girl suffered under the outrage
inflicted on her. Going to London with my recommendation, she answered the first advertisement that she saw,
and was unfortunate enough to begin her career in
domestic service in the very lodging-house, to which (as I
gather from the newspaper report of the murder) the man
Zebedee took the person whom he married, after deserting
Priscilla. Be assured that you are about to unite yourself to
an excellent girl, and accept my best wishes for your
happiness.*

It was plain from this that neither the rector nor the parents
and friends knew anything of the purchase of the knife. The
one miserable man who knew the truth, was the man who had
asked her to be his wife.

I owed it to myself – at least it seemed to me – not to let it be
supposed that I, too, had meanly deserted her. Dreadful as the
prospect was, I felt that I must see her once more, and for the
last time.

She was at work when I went into her room. As I opened
the door she started to her feet. Her cheeks reddened, and her
eyes flashed with anger. I stepped forward – and she saw my
face. My face silenced her.

I spoke in the fewest words I could find.

'I have been to the cutler's shop at Waterbank,' I said.

'There is the unfinished inscription on the knife, completed in your handwriting. I could hang you by a word. God forgive me – I can't say the word.'

Her bright complexion turned to a dreadful clay-colour. Her eyes were fixed and staring, like the eyes of a person in a fit. She stood before me, still and silent. Without saying more, I dropped the inscription into the fire. Without saying more, I left her.

I never saw her again.

8

But I heard from her a few days later.

The letter has been long since burnt. I wish I could have forgotten it as well. It sticks to my memory. If I die with my senses about me, Priscilla's letter will be my last recollection on earth.

In substance it repeated what the rector had already told me. Further, it informed me that she had bought the knife as a keepsake for Zebedee, in place of a similar knife which he had lost. On the Saturday, the banns were put up. On the Monday, she was deserted – and she snatched the knife from the table while the engraver was at work.

She only knew that Zebedee had added a new sting to the insult inflicted on her, when he arrived at the lodgings with his wife. Her duties as cook kept her in the kitchen – and Zebedee never discovered that she was in the house. I still remember the last lines of her confession:

The devil entered into me when I tried their door, on my way up to bed, and found it unlocked, and listened a while, and peeped in. I saw them by the dying light of the candle – one asleep on the bed, the other asleep by the fireside. I had the knife in my hand, and the thought came to me to do it, so that they might hang her for the murder. I couldn't take the knife out again, when I had done it. Mind this! I did really like you – I didn't say yes, because you could hardly hang your own wife, if you found out who killed Zebedee.

Since that past time I have never heard again of Priscilla Thurlby. I don't know whether she is living or dead. Many people may think I deserve to be hanged myself for not having given her up to the gallows. They may, perhaps, be disappointed when they see this confession, and hear that I have died decently in my bed. I don't blame them. I am a penitent sinner. I wish all merciful Christians goodbye for ever.

John Jago's Ghost

1

'Heart all right,' said the doctor. 'Lungs all right. No organic disease that I can discover. Philip Lefrank, don't alarm yourself. You are not going to die yet. The disease you are suffering from is – overwork. The remedy in your case is – rest.'

So the doctor spoke, in my chambers in the Temple (London), having been sent for to see me about half an hour after I had alarmed my clerk by fainting at my desk. I have no wish to intrude myself needlessly on the reader's attention; but it may be necessary to add, in the way of explanation, that I am a 'junior' barrister in good practice. I come from the Channel Island of Jersey. The French spelling of my name (Lefranc) was Anglicised generations since, in the days when the letter 'k' was still used in England at the end of words which now terminate in 'c'. We hold our heads high, nevertheless, as a Jersey family. It is to this day a trial to my father to hear his son described as a member of the English bar.

'Rest!' I repeated, when my medical adviser had done. 'My good friend, are you aware that it is term time? The courts are sitting. Look at the briefs waiting for me on that table! Rest means ruin in my case.'

'And work,' added the doctor quietly, 'means death.'

I started. He was not trying to frighten me: he was plainly in earnest.

'It is merely a question of time,' he went on. 'You have a fine constitution; you are a young man; but you cannot deliberately overwork your brain, and derange your nervous system much longer. Go away at once. If you are a sailor, take a sea-voyage. The ocean-air is the best of all air to build you up again. No: I don't want to write a prescription. I decline to physic you. I have no more to say.'

With those words my medical friend left the room. I was

obstinate: I went into court the same day.

The senior counsel in the case on which I was engaged applied to me for some information which it was my duty to give him. To my horror and amazement, I was perfectly unable to collect my ideas: facts and dates all mingled confusedly in my mind. I was led out of court thoroughly terrified about myself. The next day my briefs went back to the attorneys. I followed my doctor's advice by taking my passage for America in the first steamer that sailed for New York.

I had chosen the voyage to America in preference to any other trip by sea, with a special object in view. A relative of my mother's had emigrated to the United States many years since, and had thriven there as a farmer. He had given me a general invitation to visit him if I ever crossed the Atlantic. The long period of inaction, under the name of *rest*, to which the doctor's decision had condemned me, could hardly be more pleasantly occupied, as I thought, than by paying a visit to my relation, and seeing what I could of America in that way. After a brief sojourn at New York, I started by railway for a residence of my host – Mr Isaac Meadowcroft, of Morwick Farm.

There are some of the grandest natural prospects on the face of creation in America. There is also to be found in certain States of the Union, by way of wholesome contrast, scenery as flat, as monotonous, and as uninteresting to the traveller, as any that the earth can show. The part of the country in which Mr Meadowcroft's farm was situated fell within this latter category. I looked round me when I stepped out of the railway carriage on the platform at Morwick Station, and I said to myself, 'If to be cured means, in my case, to be dull, I have accurately picked out the very place for the purpose.'

I look back at those words by the light of later events, and I pronounce them, as you will soon pronounce them, to be the words of an essentially rash man, whose hasty judgement never stopped to consider what surprises time and chance together might have in store for him.

Mr Meadowcroft's eldest son, Ambrose, was waiting at the station to drive me to the farm.

There was no forewarning, in the appearance of Ambrose Meadowcroft, of the strange and terrible events that were to follow my arrival at Morwick. A healthy, handsome young fellow, one of thousands of other healthy, handsome young fellows, said, 'How d'ye do, Mr Lefrank? Glad to see you, sir. Jump into the buggy: the man will look after your portmanteau.' With equally conventional politeness I answered, 'Thank you. How are you all at home?' So we started on the way to the farm.

Our conversation on the drive began with the subjects of agriculture and breeding. I displayed my total ignorance of crops and cattle before we had travelled ten yards on our journey. Ambrose Meadowcroft cast about for another topic, and failed to find it. Upon this I cast about on my side, and asked, at a venture, if I had chosen a convenient time for my visit. The young farmer's stolid brown face instantly brightened. I had evidently hit, haphazard, on an interesting subject.

'You couldn't have chosen a better time,' he said. 'Our house had never been so cheerful as it is now.'

'Have you any visitors staying with you?'

'It's not exactly a visitor. It's a new member of the family who has come to live with us.'

'A new member of the family? May I ask who it is?'

Ambrose Meadowcroft considered before he replied; touched his horse with the whip; looked at me with a certain sheepish hesitation; and suddenly burst out with the truth, in the plainest possible words: 'It's just the nicest girl, sir, you ever saw in your life.'

'Ay, ay! A friend of your sister's, I suppose?'

'A friend! Bless your heart! It's our little American cousin – Naomi Colebrook.'

I vaguely remembered that a younger sister of Mr Meadowcroft's had married an American merchant in the remote past, and had died many years since, leaving an only child. I was now further informed that the father also was dead. In his last moments he had committed his helpless daughter to the compassionate care of his wife's relations at Morwick.

'He was always a speculating man,' Ambrose went on. 'Tried one thing after another, and failed in all. Died, sir, leaving barely enough to bury him. My father was a little doubtful, before she came here, how his American niece would turn out. We are English, you know, and though we do live in the United States, we stick fast to our English ways and habits. We don't much like American women in general, I can tell you. But when Naomi made her appearance, she conquered us all. Such a girl! Took her place as one of the family directly. Learnt to make herself useful in the dairy in a week's time. I tell you this: she hasn't been with us quite two months yet – and we wonder already how we ever got on without her!'

Once started on the subject of Naomi Colebrook, Ambrose held to that one topic, and talked on it without intermission. It required no great gift of penetration to discover the impression which the American cousin had produced in this case. The young fellow's enthusiasm communicated itself, in a certain tepid degree, to me. I really felt a mild flutter of anticipation at the prospect of seeing Naomi, when we drew up, towards the close of evening, at the gates of Morwick Farm.

2

Immediately on my arrival, I was presented to Mr Meadowcroft, the father.

The old man had become a confirmed invalid, confined by chronic rheumatism to his chair. He received me kindly, and a little wearily as well. His only unmarried daughter (he had long since been left a widower) was in the room, in attendance on her father. She was a melancholy, middle-aged woman, without visible attractions of any sort – one of those persons who appear to accept the obligation of living, under protest, as a burden which they would never have consented to bear if they had only been consulted first. We three had a dreary little interview in a parlour of bare walls, and then I was permitted to go upstairs, and unpack my portmanteau in my own room.

'Supper will be at nine o'clock, sir,' said Miss Meadowcroft.

She pronounced those words as if 'supper' was a form of domestic offence, habitually committed by the men, and endured by the women. I followed the groom up to my room, not overwell pleased with my first experience of the farm.

No Naomi, and no romance, thus far!

My room was clean – oppressively clean. I quite longed to see a little dust somewhere. My library was limited to the Bible and the Prayer Book. My view from the window showed me a dead flat in a partial state of cultivation, fading sadly from view in the waning light. Above the head of my spruce white bed hung a scroll, bearing a damnatory quotation from scripture in emblazoned letters of red and black. The dismal presence of Miss Meadowcroft had passed over my bedroom, and had blighted it. My spirits sank as I looked round me. Supper-time was still an event in the future. I lit the candles, and took from my portmanteau what I firmly believed to have been the first French novel ever produced at Morwick Farm. It was one of the masterly and charming stories of Dumas the elder. In five minutes I was in a new world, and my melancholy room was full of the liveliest French company. The sound of an imperative and uncompromising bell recalled me in due time to the regions of reality. I looked at my watch. Nine o'clock.

Ambrose met me at the bottom of the stairs, and showed me the way to the supper-room.

Mr Meadowcroft's invalid-chair had been wheeled to the head of the table. On his right-hand side sat his sad and silent daughter. She signed to me, with a ghostly solemnity, to take the vacant place on the left of her father. Silas Meadowcroft came in at the same moment, and was presented to me by his brother. There was a strong family likeness between them, Ambrose being the taller and handsomer man of the two. But there was no marked character in either face. I set them down as men with undeveloped qualities, waiting (the good and evil qualities alike) for time and circumstances to bring them to their full growth.

The door opened again while I was still studying the two brothers, without, I honestly confess, being very favourably impressed by either of them. A new member of the family circle, who instantly attracted my attention, entered the room.

He was short, spare, and wiry; singularly pale for a person whose life was passed in the country. The face was in other respects, beside this, a striking face to see. As to the lower part, it was covered with a thick black beard and moustache, at a time when shaving was the rule, and beards the rare exception in America. As to the upper part of the face, it was irradiated by a pair of wild, glittering brown eyes, the expression of which suggested to me that there was something not quite right with the man's mental balance. A perfectly sane person in all his sayings and doings, so far as I could see, there was still something in those wild brown eyes which suggested to me that, under exceptionally trying circumstances, he might surprise his oldest friends by acting in some exceptionally violent or foolish way. 'A little cracked' – that, in the popular phrase, was my impression of the stranger who now made his appearance in the supper-room.

Mr Meadowcroft the elder, having not spoken one word thus far, himself introduced the newcomer to me, with a side-glance at his sons, which had something like defiance in it – a glance which, as I was sorry to notice, was returned with a similar appearance of defiance by the two young men.

'Philip Lefrank, this is my overlooker, Mr Jago,' said the old man, formally presenting us. 'John Jago, this is my young relative by marriage, Mr Lefrank. He is not well! Mr Jago is an American, Philip. I hope you have no prejudice against Americans. Make acquaintance with Mr Jago. Sit together.' He cast another dark look at his sons; and the sons again returned it. They pointedly drew back from John Jago as he approached the empty chair next to me, and moved around to the opposite side of the table. It was plain that the man with the beard stood high in the father's favour, and that he was cordially disliked for that or for some other reason by the sons.

The door opened once more. A young lady quietly joined the party at the supper-table.

Was the young lady Naomi Colebrook? I looked at Ambrose, and saw the answer in his face. Naomi at last!

A pretty girl, and so far as I could judge by appearances, a good girl too. Describing her generally, I may say that she had a small head, well carried, and well set on her shoulders; bright grey eyes, that looked at you honestly, and meant what they looked; a trim, slight little figure – too slight for our English notions of beauty; a strong American accent; and (a rare thing in America) a pleasantly toned voice, which made the accent agreeable to English ears. Our first impressions of people are, in nine cases out of ten, the right impressions. I liked Naomi Colebrook at first sight; liked her pleasant smile; liked her hearty shake of the hand when we were presented to each other. 'If I get on well with nobody else in the house,' I thought to myself, 'I shall certainly get on well with *you.*'

For once in a way, I proved a true prophet. In the atmosphere of smouldering enmities at Morwick Farm, the pretty American girl and I remained firm and true friends from first to last.

Ambrose himself made room for Naomi to sit between his brother and himself. She changed colour for a moment, and looked at him, with a pretty reluctant tenderness, as she took her chair. I strongly suspected the young farmer of squeezing her hand privately, under cover of the tablecloth.

The supper was not a merry one. The only cheerful conversation was the conversation across the table between Naomi and me.

For some incomprehensible reason, John Jago seemed to be ill at ease in the presence of his young countrywoman. He looked up at Naomi doubtingly from his plate, and looked down again slowly with a frown. When I addressed him, he answered constrainedly. Even when he spoke to Mr Meadowcroft, he was still on his guard – on his guard against the two young men, as I fancied by the direction which his eyes took on these occasions. When we began our meal, I had noticed for the first time that Silas Meadowcroft's hand was strapped up with surgical plaster. I now further observed that John Jago's wandering brown eyes, furtively looking at everybody round the table in turn, looked with curious cynical scrutiny at the young man's injured hand.

By way of making my first evening at the farm all the more embarrassing to me as a stranger, I discovered before long that the father and sons were talking indirectly *at* each other, through Mr Jago and through me. When old Mr Meadowcroft spoke disparagingly to his overlooker of some past mistake made in the cultivation of the arable land of the farm, old Mr Meadowcroft's eyes pointed the application of his hostile criticism straight in the direction of his two sons. When the two sons seized a stray remark of mine about animals in general, and applied it satirically to the mismanagement of sheep and oxen in particular, they looked at John Jago while they talked to me. On occasions of this sort – and they happened frequently – Naomi struck in resolutely at the right moment, and turned the talk to some harmless topic. Every time she took a prominent part in this way in keeping the peace, melancholy Miss Meadowcroft looked slowly round at her in stern disparagement of her interference. A more dreary and more disunited family party I never sat at the table with. Envy, hatred, malice, and uncharitableness are never so essentially detestable to my mind as when they are animated by a sense of propriety, and work under the surface. But for my interest in Naomi, and my other interest in the little love-looks which I now and then surprised passing between her and Ambrose, I should never have sat through that supper. I should certainly have taken refuge in my French novel and my own room.

At last the unendurable long meal, served with ostentatious profusion, was at an end. Miss Meadowcroft rose with her ghostly solemnity, and granted me my dismissal in these words:

'We are early people at the farm, Mr Lefrank. I wish you good night.'

She laid her bony hands on the back of Mr Meadowcroft's invalid-chair, cut him short in his farewell salutation to me, and wheeled him out to his bed as if she were wheeling him out to his grave.

'Do you go to your room immediately, sir? If not, may I offer you a cigar? – provided the young gentlemen will permit it.'

So, picking his words with painful deliberation, and pointing his reference to 'the young gentlemen' with one sardonic side-look at them, Mr John Jago performed the duties of hospitality on his side. I excused myself from accepting the cigar. With studied politeness, the man of the glittering brown eyes wished me a good night's rest, and left the room.

Ambrose and Silas both approached me hospitably, with their open cigar cases in their hands.

'You were quite right to say no,' Ambrose began. 'Never smoke with John Jago. His cigars will poison you.'

'And never believe a word John Jago says to you,' added Silas. 'He is the greatest liar in America, let the other be whom he may.'

Naomi shook her forefinger reproachfully at them, as if the two sturdy young farmers had been two children.

'What will Mr Lefrank think,' she said, 'if you talk in that way of a person whom your father respects and trusts? Go and smoke. I am ashamed of both of you.'

Silas slunk away without a word of protest. Ambrose stood his ground, evidently bent on making his peace with Naomi before he left her.

Seeing that I was in the way, I walked aside towards a glass door at the lower end of the room. The door opened on the trim little farm-garden, bathed at that moment in lovely moonlight. I stepped out to enjoy the scene, and found my way to a seat under an elm tree. The grand repose of nature had never looked so unutterably solemn and beautiful as it now appeared, after what I had seen and heard inside the house. I understood, or thought I understood, the sad despair of humanity which led men into monasteries in the old time. The misanthropical side of my nature (where is the sick man who is not conscious of that side of him?) was fast getting the upper hand of me – when I felt a light touch laid on my shoulder, and found myself reconciled to my species once more by Naomi Colebrook.

3

'I want to speak to you,' Naomi began. 'You don't think ill of me for following you out here? We are not accustomed to stand much on ceremony in America.'

'You are quite right in America. Pray sit down.'

She seated herself by my side, looking at me frankly and fearlessly by the light of the moon.

'You are related to the family here,' she resumed, 'and I am related too. I guess I may say to *you* what I couldn't say to a stranger. I am right glad you have come here, Mr Lefrank, and for a reason, sir, which you don't suspect.'

'Thank you for the compliment you pay me, Miss Cole-brook, whatever the reason may be.'

She took no notice of my reply: she steadily pursued her own train of thought.

'I guess you may do some good, sir, in this wretched house,' the girl went on, with her eyes still fixed earnestly on my face. 'There is no love, no trust, no peace at Morwick Farm. They want somebody here – except Ambrose: don't think ill of Ambrose, he is only thoughtless – I say, the rest of them want somebody here to make them ashamed of their hard hearts,

43

and their horrid, false, envious ways. You are a gentleman. You know more than they know: they can't help themselves, they must look up to *you*. Try, Mr Lefrank, when you have the opportunity – pray, try, sir, to make peace among them. You heard what went on at supper-time; and you were disgusted with it. Oh, yes, you were! I saw you frown to yourself; and I know what *that* means in you Englishmen.'

There was no choice but to speak one's mind plainly to Naomi. I acknowledged the impression which had been produced on me at supper-time just as plainly as I have acknowledged it in these pages. Naomi nodded her head in undisguised approval of my candour.

'That will do; that's speaking out,' she said. 'But – oh, my! you put it a deal too mildly, sir, when you say the men don't seem to be on friendly terms together here. They hate each other. That's the word, Mr Lefrank – hate. Bitter, bitter, bitter hate!' She clenched her little fists; she shook them vehemently, by way of adding emphasis to her last words, and then she suddenly remembered Ambrose. 'Except Ambrose.' She added, opening her hand again, and laying it very earnestly on my arm. 'Don't go and misjudge Ambrose, sir. There is no harm in poor Ambrose.'

The girl's innocent frankness was really irresistible.

'Should I be altogether wrong,' I asked, 'if I guessed you were a little partial to Ambrose?'

An Englishwoman would have felt, or would at least have assumed, some little hesitation at replying to my question. Naomi did not hesitate for an instant.

'You are quite right, sir,' she said, with the most perfect composure. 'If things go well, I mean to marry Ambrose.'

'If things go well,' I repeated. 'What does that mean? Money?'

She shook her head.

'It means a fear that I have in my own mind,' she answered, 'a fear, Mr Lefrank, of matters taking a bad turn among the men here – the wicked, hard-hearted, unfeeling men. I don't mean Ambrose, sir: I mean his brother Silas, and John Jago. Did you notice Silas' hand? John Jago did that, sir, with a knife.'

'By accident?' I asked.

'On purpose,' she answered. 'In return for a blow.'

This plain revelation of the state of things at Morwick Farm rather staggered me. Blows and knives under the rich and respectable roof-tree of old Mr Meadowcroft! Blows and knives not among the labourers, but among the masters! My first impression was like *your* first impression, no doubt. I could hardly believe it.

'Are you sure of what you say?' I enquired.

'I have it from Ambrose. Ambrose would never deceive me. Ambrose knows all about it.'

My curiosity was powerfully excited. To what sort of household had I rashly voyaged across the ocean in search of rest and quiet?

'May I know all about it too?' I said.

'Well, I will try and tell you what Ambrose told me. But you must promise one thing first, sir. Promise you won't go away and leave us when you know the whole truth. Shake hands on it, Mr Lefrank. Come, shake hands on it.'

There was no resisting her fearless frankness. I shook hands on it. Naomi entered on her narrative the moment I had given her my pledge, without wasting a word by way of preface.

'When you are shown over the farm here,' she began, 'you will see that it is really two farms in one. On this side of it, as we look from under this tree, they raise crops: on the other

45

side – on much the larger half of the land, mind – they raise cattle. When Mr Meadowcroft got too old and too sick to look after the farm himself, the boys (I mean Ambrose and Silas) divided the work between them. Ambrose looked after the crops, and Silas after the cattle. Things didn't go well, somehow, under their management. I can't tell you why. I am only sure Ambrose was not in fault. The old man got more and more dissatisfied, especially about his beasts. His pride is in his beasts. Without saying a word to the boys, he looked about privately (*I* think he was wrong in that, sir; don't you?) – he looked about privately for help; and, in an evil hour, he heard of John Jago. Do you like John Jago, Mr Lefrank?'

'So far, no. I don't like him.'

'Just my sentiments, sir. But I don't know: it's likely we may be wrong. There's nothing against John Jago, except that he is so odd in his ways. They do say he wears all that nasty hair on his face (I hate hair on a man's face) on account of a vow he made when he lost his wife. Don't you think, Mr Lefrank, a man must be a little mad who shows his grief at losing his wife by vowing that he will never shave himself again? Well, that's what they do say John Jago vowed. Perhaps it's a lie. People are such liars here! Anyway, it's truth (the boys themselves confess *that*) when John came to the farm he came with a first-rate character. The old man here isn't easy to please; and he pleased the old father. Yes, that's so. Mr Meadowcroft don't like my countrymen in general. He's like his sons – English, bitter English, to the marrow of his bones. Somehow, in spite of that, John Jago got round him; maybe because John does certainly know his business. Oh, yes! Cattle and crops, John knows his business. Since he's been overlooker, things have prospered as they didn't prosper in the time of the boys. Ambrose owned as much to me himself. Still, sir, it's hard to

46

be set aside for a stranger isn't it? John gives the orders now. The boys do the work; but they have no voice in it when John and the old man put their heads together over the business of the farm. I have been long in telling you it, sir; but now you know how the envy and the hatred grew among the men, before my time. Since I have been here, things seem to get worse and worse. There's hardly a day goes by that hard words don't pass between the boys and John, or the boys and their father. The old man has an aggravating way, Mr Lefrank – a nasty way, as we do call it – of taking John Jago's part. Do speak to him about it when you get the chance. The main blame of the quarrel between Silas and John the other day lies at his door, I think. I don't want to excuse Silas, either. It was brutal of him – though he *is* Ambrose's brother – to strike John, who is the smaller and weaker man of the two. But it was worse than brutal in John, to out with his knife, and try to stab Silas. Oh, he did it! If Silas had not caught the knife in his hand (his hand's awfully cut, I can tell you: I dressed it myself), it might have ended, for anything I know, in murder –'

She stopped as the word passed her lips, looked back over her shoulder, and started violently.

I looked where my companion was looking. The dark figure of a man was standing, watching us, in the shadow of the elm tree. I rose directly to approach him. Naomi recovered her self-possession, and checked me before I could interfere.

'Who are you?' she asked, turning sharply towards the stranger. 'What do you want here?'

The man stepped out from the shadow into the moonlight, and stood revealed to us as John Jago.

'I hope I am not intruding?' he said, looking hard at me.

'What do you want?' Naomi repeated.

'I don't wish to disturb you, or to disturb this gentleman,' he

47

proceeded. 'When you are quite at leisure, Miss Naomi, you would be doing me a favour if you would permit me to say a few words to you in private.'

He spoke with the most scrupulous politeness, trying, and trying vainly, to conceal some strong agitation, which was in possession of him. His wild brown eyes – wilder than ever in the moonlight – rested entreatingly, with a strange underlying expression of despair, on Naomi's face. His hands, clasped tightly in front of him, trembled incessantly. Little as I liked the man, he did really impress me as a pitiable object at that moment.

'Do you mean that you want to speak to me tonight?' Naomi asked, in undisguised surprise.

'Yes, miss, if you please, at your leisure and at Mr Lefrank's.' Naomi hesitated.

'Won't it keep till tomorrow?' she said.

'I shall be away on farm business tomorrow, miss, for the whole day. Please to give me a few minutes this evening.' He advanced a step towards her: his voice faltered, and dropped timidly to a whisper. 'I really have something to say to you, Miss Naomi. It would be a kindness on your part – a very, very great kindness – if you will let me say it before I rest tonight.'

I rose again to resign my place to him. Once more Naomi checked me.

'No,' she said. 'Don't stir.' She addressed John Jago very reluctantly, 'If you are so much in earnest about it, Mr John, I suppose it must be. I can't guess what *you* can possibly have to say to me which cannot be said before a third person. However, it wouldn't be civil, I suppose, to say no in my place. You know it's my business to wind up the hall clock at ten every night. If you choose to come and help me, the chances are that we shall have the hall to ourselves. Will that do?'

'Not in the hall, miss, if you will excuse me.'

'Not in the hall!'

'And not in the house either, if I may make so bold.'

'What do you mean?' She turned impatiently, and appealed to me. 'Do *you* understand him?'

John Jago signed to me imploringly to let him answer for himself.

'Bear with me, Miss Naomi,' he said. 'I think I can make you understand me. There are eyes on the watch, and ears on the watch, in the house. There are some footsteps – I won't say whose – so soft, that no person can hear them.'

The last allusion evidently made itself understood. Naomi stopped him before he could say more.

'Well, where is it to be?' she asked, resignedly. 'Will the garden do, Mr John?'

'Thank you kindly, miss: the garden will do.' He pointed to a gravel-walk beyond us, bathed in the full flood of the moonlight. 'There,' he said, 'where we can see all around us, and be sure that nobody is listening. At ten o'clock.' He paused and addressed himself to me. 'I beg to apologise, sir, for intruding myself on your conversation. Please to excuse me.'

His eyes rested with a last anxious pleading look on Naomi's face. He bowed to us, and melted away into the shadow of the tree. The distant sound of a door, closed softly, came to us through the stillness of the night. John Jago had re-entered the house.

Now that he was out of hearing, Naomi spoke to me very earnestly: 'Don't suppose, sir, I have any secrets with *him*,' she said. 'I know no more than you do what he wants with me. I have half a mind not to keep the appointment. It's close on ten now. What would you do in my place?'

'Having made the appointment,' I answered, 'it seems to be due to yourself to keep it. If you feel the slightest alarm, I will wait in another part of the garden, so that I can hear if you call me.'

She received my proposal with a saucy toss of the head, and a smile of pity for my ignorance.

'You are a stranger, Mr Lefrank, or you would never talk to me in that way. In America, we don't do the men the honour of letting them alarm us. In America, the women take care of themselves. He has got my promise to meet him, as you say, and I must keep my promise. Only think,' she added, speaking more to herself than to me, 'of John Jago finding out Miss Meadowcroft's nasty, sly, underhand ways in the house! Most men would never have noticed her!'

I was completely taken by surprise. Sad and severe Miss Meadowcroft a listener and a spy! What next at Morwick Farm?

'Was that hint at the watchful eyes and ears, and the soft footsteps, really an allusion to Mr Meadowcroft's daughter?' I asked.

'Of course it was. Ah! She has imposed on you as she imposes on everybody else. The false wretch! She is secretly at the bottom of half the bad feeling among the men. I am certain of it – she keeps Mr Meadowcroft's mind bitter towards the boys. Old as she is, Mr Lefrank, and ugly as she is, she wouldn't object (if she could only make him ask her) to be John Jago's second wife. No, sir, and she wouldn't break her heart if the boys were not left a stick or stone on the farm when the father dies. I have watched her, and I know it. Ah! I could tell you such things. But there's no time now – there's ten o'clock striking! – we must say good night. I am right glad I have spoken to you, sir. I say again, at parting, what I have said already: use your influence, pray use your influence, to soften them, and to make them ashamed of themselves, in this wicked house. We will have more talk about what you can say tomorrow, when you are shown over the farm. Say goodbye now. I must keep my appointment. Look! Here is John Jago stealing out again in the shadow of the tree! Good night, friend Lefrank, and pleasant dreams.'

With one hand she took mine, and pressed it cordially; with the other hand she pushed me away without ceremony in the direction of the house. A charming girl! – an irresistible girl! I was nearly as bad as the boys, I declare, *I* almost hated John Jago, too, as we crossed each other in the shadow of the tree.

Arrived at the glass door, I stopped, and looked back at the gravel-walk.

They had met. I saw the two shadowy figures slowly pacing backwards and forwards in the moonlight, the woman a little in advance of the man. What was he saying to her? Why was he so anxious that not a word of it should be heard? Our presentiments are sometimes, in certain rare cases, the faithful prophecy of the future. A vague distrust of that moonlight-meeting stealthily took a hold on my mind. 'Will mischief come of it?' I asked myself, as I closed the door and entered the house.

Mischief *did* come of it. You shall hear how.

4

Persons of sensitive nervous temperament, sleeping for the first time in a strange house, and in a bed that is new to them, must make up their minds to pass a wakeful night. My first night at Morwick Farm was no exception to this rule. The little sleep I had was broken and disturbed by dreams. Towards six o'clock in the morning my bed became unendurable to me.

The sun was shining in brightly at the window. I determined to try the reviving influence of a stroll in the fresh morning air.

Just as I got out of bed, I heard footsteps and voices under my window.

The footsteps stopped, and the voices became recognisable. I had passed the night with my window open: I was able, without exciting notice from below, to look out.

The persons beneath me were Silas Meadowcroft, John Jago, and three strangers, whose dress and appearance indicated plainly enough that they were labourers on the farm. Silas was swinging a stout beechen stick in his hand, and was speaking to Jago, coarsely and insolently enough, of his moonlight-meeting with Naomi on the previous night.

'Next time you go courting a young lady in secret,' said Silas, 'make sure that the moon goes down first, or wait for a cloudy sky. You were seen in the garden, Master Jago; and you may as well tell us the truth for once in a way. Did you find her open to persuasion, sir? Did she say yes?'

John Jago kept his temper.

'If you must have your joke, Mr Silas,' he said, quietly and firmly, 'be pleased to joke on some other subject. You are quite wrong, sir, in what you suppose to have passed between the young lady and me.'

Silas turned about, and addressed himself ironically to the three labourers.

'You hear him, boys? He can't tell the truth, try him as you may. He wasn't making love to Naomi in the garden last night – oh, dear, no! He has had one wife already, and he knows better than to take the yoke on his shoulders for the second time!'

Greatly to my surprise, John Jago met this clumsy jesting with a formal and serious reply.

'You are quite right, sir,' he said, 'I have no intention of marrying for the second time. What I was saying to Miss Naomi doesn't matter to you. It was not at all what you choose to suppose. It was something of quite another kind, with which you have no concern. Be pleased to understand once and for all, Mr Silas, that not so much as the thought of making love to the young lady has ever entered my head. I respect her; I admire her good qualities: but if she was the only woman left in the world, and if I was a much younger man than I am, I should never think of asking her to be my wife.' He burst out suddenly into a harsh uneasy laugh. 'No, no! not my style, Mr Silas – not my style!'

Something in those words, or in his manner of speaking them, appeared to exasperate Silas. He dropped his clumsy irony, and addressed himself directly to John Jago in a tone of savage contempt.

'Not your style?' he repeated. 'Upon my soul, that's a cool way of putting it, for a man in your place! What do you mean by calling her "not your style"? You impudent beggar! Naomi Colebrook is meat for your master!'

John Jago's temper began to give way at last. He approached defiantly a step or two nearer to Silas Meadowcroft.

'Who is my master?' he asked.

'Ambrose will show you, if you go to him,' answered the other. 'Naomi is *his* sweetheart, not mine. Keep out of his way, if you want to keep a whole skin on your bones.'

John Jago cast one of his sardonic side-looks at the farmer's wounded left hand. 'Don't forget your own skin, Mr Silas, when you threaten mine! I have set my mark on you once, sir. Let me by on my business, or I may mark you for a second time.'

Silas lifted his beechen stick. The labourers, roused to some rude sense of the serious turn which the quarrel was taking, got between the two men, and parted them. I had been hurriedly dressing myself while the altercation was proceeding. Now I ran downstairs to try what my influence could do towards keeping the peace at Morwick Farm.

The war of angry words was still going on when I joined the men outside.

'Be off with you on your business, you cowardly hound!' I heard Silas say. 'Be off with you to the town! and take care you don't meet Ambrose on the way!'

'Take *you* care you don't feel my knife again before I go!' cried the other man.

Silas made a desperate effort to break away from the labourers who were holding him.

'Last time you only felt my fist!' he shouted. 'Next time you shall feel *this*!'

He lifted the stick as he spoke. I stepped up, and snatched it out of his hand.

'Mr Silas,' I said, 'I am an invalid, and I going out for a walk. Your stick will be useful to me. I beg leave to borrow it.'

The labourers burst out laughing. Silas fixed his eyes on me with a stare of angry surprise. John Jago, immediately recovering his self-possession, took off his hat, and made me a deferential bow.

'I had no idea, Mr Lefrank, that we were disturbing you,' he said. 'I am very much ashamed of myself, sir. I beg to apologise.'

'I accept your apology, Mr Jago,' I answered, 'on the understanding that you, as the older man, will set the example of forbearance, if your temper is tried on any future occasion as it has been tried today. And I have further to request,' addressing myself to Silas, 'that you will do me a favour as your father's guest. The next time your good spirits lead you into making jokes at Mr Jago's expense, don't carry them quite so far. I am sure you meant no harm, Mr Silas. Will you gratify me by saying so yourself? I want to see you and Mr Jago shake hands.'

John Jago instantly held out his hand, with an assumption of good feeling which was a little overacted, to my thinking. Silas Meadowcroft made no advance of the same friendly sort on his side.

'Let him go about his business,' said Silas. 'I won't waste any more words on him, Mr Lefrank, to please *you*. But (saving your presence) I'm damned if I take his hand!'

Further persuasion was plainly useless, addressed to such a man as this. Silas gave me no further opportunity of remonstrating with him, even if I had been inclined to do so. He turned about in sulky silence, and, retracing his steps along the path, disappeared round the next corner of the house. The labourers withdrew next, in different directions, to begin the day's work. John Jago and I were alone.

I left it to the man of the wild brown eyes to speak first.

'In half an hour's time, sir,' he said, 'I shall be going on business to Narrabee, our market-town here. Can I take any letters to the post for you? Or is there anything else that I can do in the town?'

I thanked him, and declined both proposals. He made me another deferential bow, and withdrew into the house. I mechanically followed the path, in the direction which Silas had taken before me.

Turning the corner of the house, and walking on for a little way, I found myself at the entrance to the stables, and face to face with Silas Meadowcroft once more. He had his elbows on the gate to the yard, swinging it slowly backwards and forwards, and turning and twisting a straw between his teeth.

When he saw me approaching him, he advanced a step from the gate, and made an effort to excuse himself, with a very ill grace.

'No offence, mister. Ask me what you will besides, and I'll do it for you. But don't ask me to shake hands with John Jago. I hate him too badly for that. If I touched him with one hand, sir, I tell you this, I should throttle him with the other!'

'That's your feeling towards the man, Mr Silas, is it?'

'That's my feeling, Mr Lefrank; and I'm not ashamed of it, either.'

'Is there any such place as a church in your neighbourhood?'

'Of course there is.'

'Do you ever go to it?'

'Of course I do.'

'At long intervals, Mr Silas?'

'Every Sunday, sir, without fail.'

Some third person behind me burst out laughing. Some third person had been listening to our talk. I turned around and discovered Ambrose Meadowcroft.

'I understand the drift of your catechism, though my brother doesn't,' he said. 'Don't be hard on Silas, sir. He isn't the only Christian who leaves his Christianity in the pew when he goes out of church. You will never make us friends with John Jago, try as you may. Why, what have you got there, Mr Lefrank? May I die if it isn't my stick! I have been looking for it everywhere!'

The thick beechen stick had been feeling uncomfortably heavy in my invalid hand for some time past. There was no sort of need for my keeping it any longer. John Jago was going away to Narrabee, and Silas Meadowcroft's savage temper was subdued to a sulky repose. I handed the stick back to

Ambrose. He laughed as he took it from me.

'You can't think how strange it feels, Mr Lefrank, to be without one's stick,' he said. 'A man gets used to his stick, sir, doesn't he? Are you ready for your breakfast?'

'Not just yet. I thought of taking a little walk first.'

'All right, sir. I wish I could go with you; but I have got my work to do this morning, and Silas has his work too. If you go back by the way you came, you will find yourself in the garden. If you want to go further, the wicket-gate at the end will lead you into the lane.'

Through sheer thoughtlessness, I did a very foolish thing. I turned back as I was told, and left the brothers together at the gate of the stable-yard.

5

Arrived at the garden, a thought struck me. The cheerful speech and easy manner of Ambrose plainly indicated that he was ignorant thus far of the quarrel which had taken place under my window. Silas might confess to having taken his brother's stick, and might mention whose head he had threatened with it. It was not only useless, but undesirable, that Ambrose should know of the quarrel. I retraced my steps to the stable-yard. Nobody was at the gate. I called alternately to Silas and to Ambrose. Nobody answered. The brothers had gone away to their work.

Returning to the garden, I heard a pleasant voice wishing me 'Good morning'. I looked round. Naomi Colebrook was standing at one of the lower windows of the farm. She had her working-apron on, and she was industriously brightening the knives for the breakfast-table on an old-fashioned board. A sleek black cat balanced himself on her shoulder watching the flashing motion of the knife as she passed it rapidly to and fro on the leather-covered surface of the board.

'Come here,' she said, 'I want to speak with you.'

I noticed, as I approached, that her pretty face was cloudy and anxious. She pushed the cat irritably off her shoulder: she welcomed me with only the faint reflection of her bright customary smile.

'I have seen John Jago,' she said. 'He has been hinting at something which he says happened under your bedroom window this morning. When I begged him to explain himself he only answered, "Ask Mr Lefrank: I must be off to Narrabee." What does it mean? Tell me right away, sir! I'm out of temper, and I can't wait!'

Except that I made the best instead of the worst of it, I told her what had happened under my window as plainly as I have told it here. She put down the knife that she was cleaning, and folded her hands before her, thinking.

'I wish I had never given John Jago that meeting,' she said. 'When a man asks anything of a woman, the woman, I find, mostly repents it if she says yes.'

She made that quaint reflection with a very troubled brow. The moonlight-meeting had left some unwelcome remembrances in her mind. I saw that as plainly as I saw Naomi herself.

What had John Jago said to her? I put the question with all needful delicacy, making my apologies beforehand.

'I should like to tell *you*,' she began, with a strong emphasis on the last word.

There she stopped. She turned pale, then suddenly flushed again to the deepest red. She took up the knife once more, and went on cleaning it as industriously as ever.

'I mustn't tell you,' she resumed, with her head down over the knife. 'I have promised not to tell anybody. That's the truth. Forget all about it, sir, as soon as you can. Hush! here's the spy who saw us last night on the walk, and who told Silas!'

Dreary Miss Meadowcroft opened the kitchen door. She carried an ostentatiously large prayer book. She looked at Naomi as only a jealous woman of middle age can look at a younger and prettier woman than herself.

'Prayers, Miss Colebrook,' she said, in her sourest manner. She paused, and noticed me standing under the window. 'Prayers, Mr Lefrank,' she added, with a look of devout pity, directed exclusively to my address.

'We will follow you directly, Miss Meadowcroft,' said Naomi.

'I have no desire to intrude on your secrets, Miss Cole-brook.'

With that acrid answer, our priestess took herself and her prayer book out of the kitchen. I joined Naomi, entering the room by the garden door. She met me eagerly.

'I am not quite easy about something,' she said. 'Did you tell me that you left Ambrose and Silas together?'

'Yes.'

'Suppose Silas tells Ambrose of what happened this morning?'

The same idea, as I have already mentioned, had occurred to my mind. I did my best to reassure Naomi.

'Mr Jago is out of the way,' I replied. 'You and I can put things right in his absence.'

She took my arm.

'Come into prayers,' she said. 'Ambrose will be there, and I shall find an opportunity of speaking to him.'

Neither Ambrose nor Silas was in the breakfast-room when we entered it. After waiting vainly for ten minutes, Mr Meadowcroft told his daughter to read the prayers. Miss

Meadowcroft read, thereupon, in the tone of an injured woman taking the throne of mercy by storm, and insisting on her rights. Breakfast followed; and still the brothers were absent. Miss Meadowcroft looked at her father, and said, 'From bad to worse, sir. What did I tell you?' Naomi instantly applied the antidote, 'The boys are no doubt detained over their work, uncle.' She turned to me. 'You want to see the farm, Mr Lefrank. Come and help me to find the boys.'

For more than an hour we visited one part of the farm after another, without discovering the missing men. We found them at last near the outskirts of a small wood, sitting, talking together, on the trunk of a felled tree.

Silas rose as we approached, and walked away without a word of greeting or apology, into the wood. As he got on his feet I noticed that his brother whispered something in his ear; and I heard him answer, 'All right!'

'Ambrose, does that mean you have something to keep secret from us?' asked Naomi, approaching her lover with a smile. 'Is Silas ordered to hold his tongue?'

Ambrose kicked sulkily at the loose stones lying about him. I noticed, with a certain surprise, that his favourite stick was not in his hand, and was not lying near him.

'Business,' he said, in answer to Naomi, not very graciously, 'business between Silas and me. That's what it means, if you must know.'

Naomi went on, woman-like, with her questions, heedless of the reception which they might meet with from an irritated man.

'Why were you both away at prayers and breakfast-time?' she asked next.

'We had too much to do,' Ambrose gruffly replied, 'and we were too far from the house.'

'Very odd,' said Naomi. 'This has never happened before, since I have been at the farm.'

'Well, live and learn. It has happened now.'

The tone in which he spoke would have warned any man to let him alone. But warnings which speak by implication only are thrown away on women. The woman, having still something on her mind, said it.

'Have you seen something of John Jago this morning?'

The smouldering ill-temper of Ambrose burst suddenly – why, it was impossible to guess – into a flame.

'How many more questions am I to answer?' he broke out, violently. 'Are you the parson, putting me through my catechism? I have seen nothing of John Jago, and I have got my work to get on with. Will that do for you?'

He turned with an oath, and followed his brother into the wood. Naomi's bright eyes looked up at me, flashing with indignation.

'What does he mean, Mr Lefrank, by speaking to me in that way? Rude brute! How dare he do it?' She paused: her voice, look, and manner suddenly changed. 'This has never happened before, sir. Has anything gone wrong? I declare, I shouldn't know Ambrose again, he is so changed. Say, how does it strike you?'

I made the best of a bad case.

'Something has upset his temper,' I said. 'The merest trifle, Miss Colebrook, upsets a man's temper sometimes. I speak as a man, and I know it. Give him time, and he will make his excuses, and all will be well again.'

My presentation of the case entirely failed to reassure my pretty companion. We went back to the house. Dinner-time came, and the brothers appeared. Their father spoke to them of their absence from morning prayers – with needless severity, as I thought. They resented the reproof with needless indignation on their side, and left the room. A sour smile of satisfaction showed itself on Miss Meadowcroft's thin lips. She looked at her father, then raised her eyes sadly to the ceiling, and said, 'We can only pray for them, sir.'

Naomi disappeared after dinner. When I saw her again, she had some news for me.

'I have been with Ambrose,' she said, 'and he has begged my pardon. We have made it up, Mr Lefrank. Still – still –'

'Still – *what*, Miss Naomi?'

'He is not like himself, sir. He denies it. But I can't help thinking he is hiding something from me.'

The day wore on: the evening came. I returned to my French novel. But not even Dumas himself could keep my attention to the story. What else I was thinking of I cannot say. Why I was out of spirits I am unable to explain. I wished myself back in England: I took a blind unreasonable hatred to Morwick Farm.

Nine o'clock struck, and we all assembled again at supper, with the exception of John Jago. He was expected back to supper, and we waited for him a quarter of an hour, by Mr Meadowcroft's own directions. John Jago never appeared.

The night wore on, and still the absent man failed to return. Miss Meadowcroft volunteered to sit up for him. Naomi eyed her, a little maliciously I must own, as the two women parted for the night. I withdrew to my room, and again I was unable to sleep. When sunrise came, I went out, as before, to breathe the morning air.

On the staircase I met Miss Meadowcroft ascending to her own room. Not a curl of her stiff grey hair was disarranged: nothing about the impenetrable woman betrayed that she had been watching through the night.

'Has Mr Jago not returned?' I asked.

Miss Meadowcroft slowly shook her head, and frowned at me.

'We are in the hands of Providence, Mr Lefrank. Mr Jago must have been detained for the night at Narrabee.'

The daily routine of the meals resumed its unalterable course. Breakfast-time came and dinner-time came, and no John Jago darkened the doors of Morwick Farm. Mr Meadowcroft and his daughter consulted together, and determined to send in search of the missing man. One of the more intelligent of the labourers was despatched to Narrabee to make enquiries.

The man returned late in the evening, bringing startling news to the farm. He had visited all the inns and all the places of business resort in Narrabee, he had made endless enquiries in every direction, with this result – no one had set eyes on John Jago. Everybody declared that John Jago had not entered the town. We all looked at each other, excepting the two brothers, who were seated together in a dark corner of the room. The conclusion appeared to be inevitable. John Jago was a lost man.

6

Mr Meadowcroft was the first to speak.

'Somebody must find John,' he said.

'Without losing a moment,' added his daughter.

Ambrose suddenly stepped out of the dark corner of the room.

'I will enquire,' he said.

Silas followed him.

'I will go with you,' he added.

Mr Meadowcroft interposed his authority.

'One of you will be enough, for the present, at least. You go, Ambrose. Your brother may be wanted later. If any accident has happened (which God forbid), we may have to enquire in more than one direction. Silas, you will stay at the farm.'

The brothers withdrew together – Ambrose to prepare for his journey, Silas to saddle one of the horses for him. Naomi slipped out after them: left in company with Mr Meadowcroft and his daughter (both devoured by anxiety about the missing man, and both trying to conceal it under an assumption of devout resignation to circumstances), I need hardly add that I too, retired, as soon as it was politely possible for me to leave the room. Ascending the stairs on my way to my own quarters, I discovered Naomi half-hidden in a recess formed by an old-fashioned window-seat on the first landing. My bright little friend was in sore trouble. Her apron was over her face, and she was crying bitterly. Ambrose had not taken his leave as tenderly as usual. She was more firmly persuaded than ever that 'Ambrose was hiding something from her'. The next day made the mystery deeper than ever. The horse which had taken Ambrose to Narrabee was ridden back to the farm by a groom from the hotel. He delivered a written message from Ambrose which startled us. Further enquiries had positively proved that the missing man had never been near Narrabee. The only attainable tidings of his whereabouts were derived from vague report. It was said that a man like John Jago had been seen the previous day in a railway car, travelling on the line to New York. Acting on this imperfect information, Ambrose had decided on verifying the truth of the report by extending his enquiries to New York.

This extraordinary proceeding forced the suspicion on me that something had really gone wrong. I kept my doubts to myself; but I was prepared, from that moment, to see the disappearance of John Jago followed by very grave results.

The same day the results declared themselves.

Time enough had now elapsed for report to spread through the district the news of what had happened at the farm. Already aware of the bad feeling existing between the men, the neighbours had been now informed (no doubt by the labourers present) of the deplorable scene that had taken place under my bedroom window. Public opinion declares itself in America without the slightest reserve, or the slightest care for consequences. Public opinion declared on this occasion that the lost man was the victim of foul play, and held one or both of the brothers Meadowcroft responsible for his disappearance. Later in the day, the reasonableness of this serious view of the case was confirmed in the popular mind by a startling discovery. It was announced that a Methodist preacher lately settled at Morwick, and greatly respected throughout the district, had dreamed of John Jago in the character of a murdered man whose bones were hidden at Morwick Farm. Before night the cry was general for a verification of the preacher's dream. Not only in the immediate district, but in the town of Narrabee itself, the public voice insisted on the necessity of a search for the mortal remains of John Jago at Morwick Farm.

In the terrible turn which matters had now taken, Mr Meadowcroft displayed a spirit and energy for which I was not prepared.

'My sons have their faults,' he said, 'serious faults, and nobody knows it better than I do. My sons have behaved badly and ungratefully towards John Jago; I don't deny that either. But Ambrose and Silas are not murderers. Make your search. I ask for it. No, I insist on it, after what had been said, in justice to my family and my name!'

The neighbours took him at his word. The Morwick section of the American nation organised itself on the spot. The sovereign people met in committee, made speeches, elected competent persons to represent the public interests, and began the search the next day. The whole proceeding, ridiculously informal from a legal point of view, was carried out by these extraordinary people with as stern and strict a sense of duty as if it had been sanctioned by the highest tribunal in the land.

Naomi met the calamity that had fallen on the household as resolutely as her uncle himself. The girl's courage rose with the call which was made on it. Her one anxiety was for Ambrose.

'He ought to be here,' she said to me. 'The wretches in this neighbourhood are wicked enough to say that his absence is a confession of his guilt.'

She was right. In the present temper of the popular mind the absence of Ambrose was a suspicious circumstance in itself.

'We might telegraph to New York,' I suggested, 'if you only knew where a message would be likely to find him.'

'I know the hotel which the Meadowcrofts use at New York,' she replied. 'I was sent there at my father's death, to wait till Miss Meadowcroft could take me to Morwick.'

We decided on telegraphing the hotel. I was writing the message, and Naomi was looking over my shoulder, when we were startled by a strange voice speaking close behind us.

'Oh! that's his address, is it?' said the voice. 'We wanted his address rather badly.'

The speaker was a stranger to me. Naomi recognised him as one of the neighbours.

'What do you want his address for?' she asked, sharply.

'I guess we've found the mortal remains of John Jago, miss,' the man replied. 'We have got Silas already, and we want Ambrose, too, on suspicion of murder.'

'It's a lie!' cried Naomi, furiously, 'a wicked lie!'

The man turned to me.

'Take her into the next room, mister,' he said, 'and let her see for herself.'

We went together into the next room.

In one corner, sitting by her father, and holding his hand, we saw stern and stony Miss Meadowcroft, weeping silently. Opposite to them, crouched on the window-seat – his eyes wandering, his hands hanging helpless – we next discovered Silas Meadowcroft, plainly self-betrayed as a panic-stricken man. A few of the persons who had been engaged in the search were seated near, watching him. The mass of the strangers present stood congregated round a table in the middle of the room. They drew aside as I approached with Naomi, and allowed us to have a clear view of certain objects placed on the table.

The centre object of the collection was a little heap of charred bones. Round this were ranged a knife, two metal buttons, and a stick partially burnt. The knife was recognised by the labourers as the weapon John Jago habitually carried about with him – the weapon with which he had wounded Silas Meadowcroft's hand. The buttons Naomi herself declared to have a peculiar pattern on them, which had formerly attracted her attention to John Jago's coat. As for the stick, burnt as it was, I had no difficulty in identifying the quaintly carved knob at the top. It was the heavy beechen stick which I had restored to Ambrose on his claiming it as his own. In reply to my enquiries, I was informed that the bones, the knife, the buttons and the stick, had all been found together in a limekiln then in use on the farm.

'Is it serious?' Naomi whispered to me, as we drew back from the table.

It would have been sheer cruelty to deceive her now.

'Yes,' I whispered back, 'it *is* serious.'

The search committee conducted its proceedings with the strictest regularity. The proper applications were made forthwith to a justice of the peace, and the justice issued his warrant. That night Silas was committed to prison, and an officer was despatched to arrest Ambrose in New York.

For my part, I did the little I could to make myself useful. With the silent sanction of Mr Meadowcroft and his daughter, I went to Narrabee, and secured the best legal assistance for the defence which the town could place at my disposal. This done, there was no choice but to wait for news of Ambrose, and for the examination before the magistrate which was to follow. I shall pass over the misery in the house during the interval of expectation: no useful purpose could be served by describing it now. Let me only say that Naomi's conduct strengthened me in the conviction that she possessed a noble nature. I was unconscious of the state of my own feelings at the time; but I am now disposed to think that this was the epoch at which I began to envy Ambrose the wife whom he had won.

The telegraph brought us our first news of Ambrose. He had been arrested at the hotel, and he was on his way to Morwick. The next day he arrived, and followed his brother to prison. The two were confined in separate cells, and were forbidden all communication with each other.

Two days later, the preliminary examination took place. Ambrose and Silas Meadowcroft were charged before the magistrate with the wilful murder of John Jago. I was cited to appear as one of the witnesses, and, at Naomi's own request,

I took the poor girl into court, and sat by her during the proceedings. My host also was present in his invalid-chair, with his daughter by his side.

Such was the result of my voyage across the ocean in search of rest and quiet, and thus did time and chance fulfil my first hasty forebodings of the dull life I was to lead at Morwick Farm!

7

On our way to the chairs allotted to us in the magistrate's court, we passed the platform on which the prisoners were standing together.

Silas took no notice of us. Ambrose made a friendly sign of recognition, and then rested his hand on the 'bar' in front of him. As she passed beneath him, Naomi was just tall enough to reach his hand on tiptoe. She took it. 'I know you are innocent,' she whispered, and gave him one look of loving encouragement as she followed me to her place. Ambrose never lost his self-control. I may have been wrong, but I thought this a bad sign.

The case, as stated for the prosecution, told strongly against the suspected men.

Ambrose and Silas Meadowcroft were charged with the murder of John Jago (by means of the stick or by use of some other weapon), and with the deliberate destruction of the body by throwing it into the quicklime. In proof of this latter assertion, the knife which the deceased habitually carried about him, and the metal buttons which were known to belong to his coat, were produced. It was argued that these inde-structible substances, and some fragments of the larger bones, had alone escaped the action of the burning lime. Having produced medical witnesses to support this theory by

declaring the bones to be human, and having thus circum-
stantially asserted the discovery of the remains in the kiln, the
prosecution next proceeded to prove that the missing man had
been murdered by the two brothers, and had been by them
thrown into the quicklime as a means of concealing their guilt.

Witness after witness deposed to the inveterate enmity
against the deceased displayed by Ambrose and Silas. The
threatening language they habitually used towards him; their
violent quarrels with him, which had become a public scandal
throughout the neighbourhood, and which had ended (on one
occasion at least) in a blow; the disgraceful scene which had
taken place under my window; and the restoration to
Ambrose, on the morning of the fatal quarrel, of the very stick
which had been found among the remains of the dead man –
these facts and events, and a host of minor circumstances
besides, sworn to by witnesses whose credit was unim-
peachable, pointed with terrible directness to the conclusion
at which the prosecution had arrived.

I looked at the brothers as the weight of the evidence
pressed more and more heavily against them. To outward
view, at least, Ambrose still maintained his self-possession. It
was far otherwise with Silas. Abject terror showed itself in his
ghastly face; in his great knotty hands, clinging convulsively to
the bar at which he stood; in his staring eyes, fixed in vacant
horror on each witness who appeared. Public feeling judged
him on the spot. There he stood, self-betrayed already, in the
popular opinion, as a guilty man!

The one point gained in cross-examination by the defence
related to the charred bones.

Pressed on this point, a majority of the medical witnesses
admitted that their examination had been a hurried one, and
that it was just possible that the bones might yet prove to be

the remains of an animal, and not of a man. The presiding magistrate decided upon this, that a second examination should be made, and that the number of the medical experts should be increased.

Here the preliminary proceedings ended. The prisoners were remanded for three days.

The prostration of Silas at the close of the enquiry was so complete that it was found necessary to have two men to support him on his leaving the court. Ambrose leaned over the bar to speak to Naomi before he followed the gaoler out.

'Wait,' he whispered confidently, ''till they hear what I have to say!' Naomi kissed her hand to him affectionately, and turned to me with the bright tears in her eyes.

'Why don't they hear what he has to say at once?' she asked. 'Anybody can see that Ambrose is innocent. It's a crying shame, sir, to send him back to prison. Don't you think so yourself?'

If I confessed what I really thought, I should have said that Ambrose had proved nothing to my mind, except that he possessed rare powers of self-control. It was impossible to acknowledge this to my little friend. I diverted her mind from the question of her lover's innocence by proposing that we should get the necessary order and visit him in his prison on the next day. Naomi dried her tears, and gave me a little grateful squeeze of the hand.

'Oh, my! what a good fellow you are!' cried the outspoken American girl. 'When your time comes to be married, sir, I guess the woman won't repent saying yes to *you*!'

Mr Meadowcroft preserved unbroken silence as we walked back to the farm on either side of his invalid-chair. His last reserves of resolution seemed to have given way under the overwhelming strain laid on them by the proceedings in court.

His daughter, in stern indulgence to Naomi, mercifully permitted her opinion to glimmer on us only, through the medium of quotation from scripture texts. If the texts meant anything, they meant that she had foreseen all that had happened, and that the one sad aspect of the case, to her mind, was the death of John Jago, unprepared to meet his end.

I obtained the order of admission to the prison the next morning.

We found Ambrose still confident of the favourable result, for his brother and for himself, of the enquiry before the magistrate. He seemed to be almost as eager to tell, as Naomi was to hear, the true story of what had happened at the limekiln. The authorities of the prison – present, of course, at the interview – warned him to remember that what he said might be taken down in writing and produced against him in court.

'Take it down, gentlemen, and welcome,' Ambrose replied. 'I have nothing to fear. I am only telling the truth.'

With that he turned to Naomi, and began his narrative, as nearly as I can remember, in these words:

'I may as well make a clean breast of it at starting, my girl. After Mr Lefrank left us that morning, I asked Silas how he came by my stick. In telling me how, Silas also told me the words that had passed between him and John Jago under Mr Lefrank's window. I was angry and jealous, and I own it freely, Naomi, I thought the worst that could be thought about you and John.'

Here Naomi stopped him without ceremony.

'Was that what made you speak to me as you spoke to me when we found you at the wood?' she asked.

'Yes.'

'And was that what made you leave me, when you went

away to Narrabee, without giving me a kiss at parting?'

'It was.'

'Beg my pardon for it before you say a word more.'

'I beg your pardon.'

'Say you are ashamed of yourself.'

'I am ashamed of myself,' Ambrose answered, penitently.

'Now you may go on,' said Naomi. 'Now I'm satisfied.'

Ambrose went on.

'We were on our way to the clearing at the other side of the wood while Silas was talking to me; and, as ill luck would have it, we took the path that led by the limekiln. Turning the corner, we met John Jago on his way to Narrabee. I was too angry, I tell you, to let him pass quietly. I gave him a bit of my mind. His blood was up too, I suppose; and he spoke out, on his side, as freely as I did. I own I threatened him with the stick; but I'll swear to it I meant him no harm. You know – after dressing Silas' hand – that John Jago is ready with his knife. He comes from out West, where they are always ready with one weapon or another handy in their pockets. It's likely enough *he* didn't mean to harm me, either – but how could I be sure of that? When he stepped up to me, and showed his weapon, I dropped the stick, and closed with him. With one hand I wrenched the knife away from him, and with the other I caught him by the collar of his rotten old coat, and gave him a shaking that made his bones rattle in his skin. A big piece of the cloth came away in my hand. I shied it into the quicklime close by us, and I pitched the knife after the cloth. If Silas hadn't stopped me, I think it's likely I might have shied John Jago himself into the lime next. As it was, Silas kept hold of me. Silas shouted out to him, "Be off with you! And don't come back again, if you don't want to be burnt in the kiln!" He stood looking at us for a minute, fetching his breath, and holding his torn coat round him. Then he spoke with a deadly quiet voice and a deadly quiet look. "Many a true word, Mr Silas," he says, "is spoken in jest. *I shall not come back again.*" He turned about, and left us. We stood staring at each other like a couple of fools. "You don't think he means it?" I says. "Bosh!" says Silas. "He's too sweet on Naomi not to come back." What's the matter now, Naomi?'

I had noticed it too. She started and turned pale when Ambrose repeated to her what Silas had said to him.

'Nothing is the matter,' Naomi answered. 'Your brother has no right to take liberties with my name. Go on. Did Silas say any more while he was about it?'

'Yes: he looked into the kiln, and he says, "What made you throw away the knife, Ambrose?" – "How does a man know why he does anything," I says, "when he does it in a passion?" – "It's a ripping-good knife," says Silas, "in your place, I should have kept it." I picked up the stick off the ground. "Who says I've lost it yet?" I answered him; and with that I got up on the side of the kiln, and began sounding for the knife, to bring it, you know, by means of the stick, within easy reach of a shovel, or some such thing. "Give us your hand," I says to Silas. "Let me stretch out a bit, and I'll have it in no time." Instead of finding the knife, I came nigh to falling myself into the burning lime. The vapour overpowered me, I suppose. All I know is, I turned giddy, and dropped the stick in the kiln. I should have followed the stick, to a dead certainty, but for Silas pulling me back by the hand. "Let it be," says Silas. "If I hadn't had hold of you, John Jago's knife might have been the death of you, after all!" He led me away by the arm, and we went on together on the road to the wood. We stopped where you found us, and sat down on the felled tree. We had a little more talk about John Jago. It ended in our agreeing to wait and see what happened, and to keep our own counsel in the meantime. You and Mr Lefrank came upon us, Naomi, while we were still talking; and you guessed right when you guessed that we had a secret from you. You know the secret now.'

There he stopped. I put the question to him – the first that I had asked yet.

'Had you or your brother any fear at that time of the charge which has since been brought against you?' I said.

'No such thought entered our heads, sir,' Ambrose answered. 'How could *we* foresee that the neighbours would search the kiln, and say what they have said of us? All we feared was that the old man might hear of the quarrel, and be bitterer against us than ever. I was the more anxious of the two to keep things secret, because I had Naomi to consider as well as the old man. Put yourself in my place, and you will own, sir, that the prospect at home was not a pleasant one for *me*, if John Jago really kept away from the farm, and if it came out that it was all my doing.'

(This was certainly an explanation of his conduct; but it was not quite satisfactory to my mind.)

'As *you* believe, then,' I went on, 'John Jago has carried out his threat of not returning to the farm? According to you, he is now alive and in hiding somewhere?'

'Certainly!' said Ambrose.

'Certainly!' repeated Naomi.

'Do you believe the report that he was seen travelling on the railway to New York?'

'I believe it firmly, sir. And, what is more, I believe I was on his track. I was only too anxious to find him – and I say I could have found him, if they would have let me stay in New York.' I looked at Naomi.

'I believe it too,' she said. 'John Jago is keeping away.'

'Do you suppose that he is afraid of Ambrose and Silas?'

She hesitated.

'He *may* be afraid of them,' she replied, with a strong emphasis on the word 'may'.

'But you don't think it likely?'

She hesitated again. I pressed her again.

'Do you think there is any other motive for his absence?'

Her eyes dropped to the floor. She answered obstinately, almost doggedly, 'I can't say.'

I addressed myself to Ambrose.

'Have you anything more to tell us?' I asked.

'No,' he said. 'I have told you all I know about it.'

I rose to speak to the lawyer whose services I had retained. He had helped us to get the order of admission, and he had accompanied us to the prison. Seated apart, he had kept silence throughout, attentively watching the effect of Ambrose Meadowcroft's narrative on the officers of the prison and on me.

'Is this the defence?' I enquired, in a whisper.

'This is the defence, Mr Lefrank. What do you think between ourselves?'

'Between ourselves, I think the magistrate will commit them for trial.'

'On the charge of murder?'

'Yes, on the charge of murder.'

8

My replies to the lawyer accurately expressed the conviction in my mind. The narrative related by Ambrose had all the appearance, to my mind, of a fabricated story, got up, and clumsily got up, to pervert the plain meaning of the circumstantial evidence produced by the prosecution. I reached this conclusion reluctantly and regretfully, for Naomi's sake. I said all I could to shake the absolute confidence which she felt in the discharge of the prisoners at the next examination.

The day of the adjourned enquiry arrived.

Naomi and I again attended the court together. Mr Meadowcroft was unable, on this occasion, to leave the house. His daughter was present, walking to the court by herself, and occupying a seat by herself.

On his second appearance at the 'bar', Silas was more composed, and more like his brother: no new witnesses were called by the prosecution. We began the battle over the medical evidence relating to the charred bones. To some extent, we won the victory. In other words we forced the doctors to acknowledge that they differed widely in their opinions. They confessed that they were not certain. Two went still further, and declared that the bones were the bones of an animal, not of a man. We made the most of this; and then we entered upon the defence, founded on Ambrose Meadowcroft's story.

Necessarily, no witnesses could be called on our side. Whether this circumstance discouraged him, or whether he privately shared my opinion of his client's statement, I cannot say – it is only certain that the lawyer spoke mechanically, doing his best, no doubt, but doing it without genuine conviction, or earnestness on his own part. Naomi cast an anxious glance at me as he sat down. The girl's hand, when I took it, turned cold in mine. She saw plain signs of the failure of the defence in the look and manner of the counsel for the prosecution; but she waited resolutely until the presiding magistrate announced his decision. I had only too clearly foreseen what he would feel it to be his duty to do. Naomi's head dropped on my shoulder as he said the terrible words which committed Ambrose and Silas Meadowcroft to take their trial on charge of murder.

I led her out of the court into the air. As I passed the 'bar', I saw Ambrose, deadly pale, looking after us as we left him; the magistrate's decision had evidently daunted him. His brother Silas had dropped in abject terror on the gaoler's chair; the miserable wretch shook and shuddered dumbly like a cowed dog.

Miss Meadowcroft returned with us to the farm, preserving unbroken silence on the way back. I could detect nothing in her bearing which suggested any compassionate feeling for the prisoners in her stern and secret nature. On Naomi's withdrawal to her own room, we were left together for a few minutes – and then, to my astonishment, the outwardly merciless woman showed me that she, too, was one of Eve's daughters, and could feel and suffer, in her own hard way, like the rest of us. She suddenly stepped close up to me, and laid her hand on my arm.

'You are a lawyer, ain't you?' she asked.

'Yes.'

'Have you had any experience in your profession?'

'Ten years' experience.'

'Do *you* think –' She stopped abruptly, her hard face softened, her eyes dropped to the ground. 'Never mind,' she said, confusedly. 'I'm upset by all this misery, though I may not look like it. Don't notice me.'

She turned away. I waited, in the firm persuasion that the unspoken question in her mind would sooner or later force its way to utterance by her lips. I was right. She came back to me unwillingly, like a woman acting under some influence which the utmost exertion of her will was powerless to resist.

'Do *you* believe John Jago is still a living man?'

She put the question vehemently, desperately, as if the

words rushed out of her mouth in spite of her.

'I do not believe it,' I answered.

'Remember what John Jago has suffered at the hands of my brothers,' she persisted. 'Is it not in your experience that he should take a sudden resolution to leave the farm?'

I replied, as plainly as before, 'It is *not* in my experience.'

She stood looking at me for a moment with a face of blank despair, then bowed her grey head in silence, and left me. As she crossed the room to the door, I saw her look upward, and I heard her say to herself softly, between her teeth, 'Vengeance is mine, I will repay, saith the Lord.'

It was the requiem of John Jago, pronounced by the woman who loved him.

When I next saw her, her mask was on once more. Miss Meadowcroft was herself again. Miss Meadowcroft could sit by, impenetrably calm, while the lawyers discussed the terrible position of her brothers, with the scaffold in view as one of the possibilities of the 'case'.

Left by myself, I began to feel uneasy about Naomi. I went upstairs, and, knocking softly at her door, made my enquiries from outside. The clear young voice answered me sadly, 'I am trying to bear it: I won't distress you when we meet again.' I descended the stairs, feeling my first suspicion of the true nature of my interest in the American girl. Why had her answer brought the tears into my eyes? I went out walking, alone, to think undisturbedly. Why did the tones of her voice dwell on my ear all the way? Why did my hand still feel the last cold faint pressure of her fingers when I led her out of court?

I took a sudden resolution to go back to England.

When I returned to the farm, it was evening. The lamp was not yet lit in the hall. Pausing to accustom my eyes to the obscurity indoors, I heard the voice of the lawyer whom we had employed for the defence, speaking to someone very earnestly.

'I'm not to blame,' said the voice. 'She snatched the paper out of my hand before I was aware of her.'

'Do you want it back?' asked the voice of Miss Meadowcroft.

'No: it's only a copy. If keeping it will help to quiet her, let her keep it by all means. Good evening.'

Saying those last words, the lawyer approached me on his way out of the house. I stopped him without ceremony: I felt an ungovernable curiosity to know more.

'Who snatched the paper out of your hand?' I asked, bluntly.

The lawyer started. I had taken him by surprise. The instinct of professional reticence made him pause before he answered me.

In the brief interval of silence, Miss Meadowcroft replied to my question from the other end of the hall.

'Naomi Colebrook snatched the paper out of his hand.'

'What paper?'

A door opened softly behind me. Naomi herself appeared on the threshold. Naomi herself answered my question.

'I will tell you,' she whispered. 'Come in here.'

One candle only was burning in the room. I looked at her by the dim light. My resolution to return to England instantly became the last one of the lost ideas of my life.

'Good God!' I exclaimed, 'what has happened now?'

She gave me the paper which she had taken from the lawyer's hand.

The 'copy' to which he had referred was a copy of the written confession of Silas Meadowcroft on his return to prison. He accused his brother Ambrose of the murder of

John Jago. He declared on his oath that he had seen his brother Ambrose commit the crime.

In the popular phrase, I could 'hardly believe my own eyes'. I read the last sentences of the confession for the second time:

I heard their voices at the limekiln. They were having words about Cousin Naomi. I ran to the place to part them. I was not in time. I saw Ambrose strike the deceased a terrible blow on the head with his (Ambrose's) heavy stick. The deceased dropped without a cry. I put my hand on his heart. He was dead. I was horribly frightened. Ambrose threatened to kill me next if I said a word to any living soul. He took up the body and cast it into the quicklime, and threw the stick in after it. We went on together to the wood. We sat down on a felled tree outside the wood. Ambrose made up the story that we were to tell if what he had done was found out. He made me repeat it after him like a lesson. We were still at it when Cousin Naomi and Mr Lefrank came up to us. They know the rest. This, on my oath, is a true confession. I make it of my own free will, repenting me sincerely that I did not make it before.

(Signed)
Silas Meadowcroft

I laid down the paper, and looked at Naomi once more. She spoke to me with a strange composure. Immovable determination was in her eye, immovable determination was in her voice.

'Silas has lied away his brother's life to save himself,' she said. 'I see cowardly falsehood and cowardly cruelty in every line on that paper. Ambrose is innocent, and the time has come to prove it.'

'You forget,' I said, 'that we have just failed to prove it.'

She took no notice of my objection.

'John Jago is alive, in hiding from us,' she went on. 'Help me, friend Lefrank, to advertise for him in the newspapers.'

I drew back from her in speechless distress. I own I believed that the new misery which had fallen on her had affected her brain.

'You don't believe it?' she said. 'Shut the door.'

I obeyed her. She seated herself, and pointed to a chair near her.

'Sit down,' she proceeded. 'I am going to do a wrong thing, but there is no help for it. I am going to break a sacred promise. You remember that moonlight night when I met him on the garden-walk?'

'John Jago?'

'Yes. Now listen. I am going to tell you what passed between John Jago and me.'

9

I waited in silence for the disclosure that was now to come. Naomi began by asking me a question.

'You remembered when we went to see Ambrose in prison?' she said.

'Perfectly.'

'Ambrose told us of something which his villain of a brother said of John Jago and me. Do you remember what it was?'

I remembered perfectly. Silas had said, 'John Jago is too sweet on Naomi not to come back.'

'That's so,' Naomi remarked, when I had repeated the words. 'I couldn't help starting when I heard what Silas had said; and I thought you noticed me.'

'I did notice you.'

'Did you wonder what it meant?'

'Yes.'

'I'll tell you. It meant this: what Silas Meadowcroft said to his brother of John Jago, was what I myself was thinking of John Jago at that very moment. It startled me to find my own thought in a man's mind, spoken for me by a man. I am the person, sir, who has driven John Jago away from Morwick Farm, and I am the person who can and will bring him back again.'

There was something in her manner, more than in her words, which let the light in suddenly on my mind.

'You have told me the secret,' I said. 'John Jago is in love with you.'

'Mad about me!' she rejoined, dropping her voice to a whisper. 'Stark, staring mad! That's the only word for him. After we had taken a few turns on the gravel-walk, he suddenly broke out like a man beside himself. He fell down on his knees; he kissed my gown, he kissed my feet; he sobbed and cried for love of me. I'm not badly off for courage, sir, considering I'm a woman. No man, that I can call to mind, ever really scared me before. But, I own, John Jago frightened me: oh, my! he did frighten me! My heart was in my mouth, and my knees shook under me. I begged and prayed of him to get up and go away. No; there he knelt, and held by the skirt of my gown. The words poured out from him like – well, like nothing I can think of but water from a pump. His happiness and his life, and his hopes in earth and heaven, and Lord only knows what besides, all depended, he said, on a word from me. I plucked up spirit enough at that to remind him that I was promised to Ambrose. "I think you ought to be ashamed of yourself," I said, "to own that you are wicked enough to love me when you know I am promised to another man!" When I

83

spoke to him, he took a new turn: he began abusing Ambrose. *That* straightened me up. I snatched my gown out of his hand, and I gave him my whole mind. "I hate you!" I said. "Even if I wasn't promised to Ambrose, I wouldn't marry you. No! Not if there wasn't another man left in the world to ask me. I hate you, Mr Jago! I hate you!" He saw I was in earnest at last. He got up from my feet, and he settled down quiet again, all of a sudden. "You have said enough" (that was how he answered me). "You have broken my life. I have no hopes and no prospects now. I had a pride in the farm, miss, and a pride in my work; I bore with your brutish cousins' hatred of me; I was faithful to Mr Meadowcroft's interests; all for your sake, Naomi Colebrook – all for your sake! I have done with it now. I have done with my life at the farm. You will never be troubled by me again. I am going away, as the dumb creatures go when they are sick, to hide myself in a corner, and die. Do me one last favour. Don't make me the laughing-stock of the whole neighbourhood. I can't bear that: it maddens me, only to think of it. Give me your promise never to tell any living soul what I have said to you tonight – your sacred promise to the man whose life you have broken!" I did as he bade me: I gave him my sacred promise with the tears in my eyes. Yes, that is so. After telling him I hated him (and I did hate him), I cried over his misery, I did. Mercy, what fools women are! What is the horrid perversity, sir, which makes us always ready to pity the men? He held out his hand to me, and he said, "Goodbye for ever!" and I pitied him. I said, "I'll shake hands with you if you will give me your promise in exchange for mine. I beg of you not to leave the farm. What will my uncle do if you go away? Stay here and be friends with me; and forget and forgive, Mr John." He gave me his promise (he can refuse me nothing), and he gave it again when I saw him again the next morning.

Yes, I'll do him justice, though I do hate him! I believe he honestly meant to keep his word as long as my eye was on him. It was only when he was left to himself that the devil tempted him to break his promise, and leave the farm. I was brought up to believe in the devil, Mr Lefrank, and I find it explains many things. It explains John Jago. Only let me find out where he has gone, and I'll engage he shall come back and clear Ambrose of the suspicion which his vile brother has cast on him. Here is the pen all ready for you. Advertise for him, friend Lefrank, and do it right away, for my sake!'

I let her run on, without attempting to dispute her conclusions, until she could say no more. When she put the pen into my hand, I began the composition of the advertisement, as obediently as if I, too, believed that John Jago was a living man.

In the case of anyone else, I should have openly acknowledged that my own convictions remained unshaken. If no quarrel had taken place at the limekiln, I should have been quite ready, as I viewed the case, to believe that John Jago's disappearance was referable to the terrible disappointment which Naomi had inflicted upon him. The same morbid dread of ridicule which had led him to assert that he cared nothing for Naomi, when he and Silas had quarrelled under my bedroom window, might also have impelled him to withdraw himself secretly and suddenly from the scene of his discomfiture. But to ask me to believe, after what had happened at the limekiln, that he was still living, was to ask me to take Ambrose Meadowcroft's statement for granted as a true statement of facts.

I had refused to do this from the first; and I still persisted in taking that course. If I had been called upon to decide the balance of probability between the narrative related by

Ambrose in his defence and the narrative related by Silas in his confession, I must have owned, no matter how unwillingly, that the confession was, to my mind, the least incredible story of the two.

Could I say this to Naomi? I would have written fifty advertisements enquiring for John Jago rather than say it; and you would have done the same, if you had been so fond of her as I was.

I drew out the advertisement, for insertion in *The Morwick Mercury*, in these terms:

> *MURDER. Printers of newspapers throughout the United States are desired to publish that Ambrose Meadowcroft and Silas Meadowcroft, of Morwick Farm, Morwick Country, are committed for trial on the charge of murdering John Jago, now missing from the farm and from the neighbourhood. Any person who can give information of the existence of said Jago may save the lives of two wrongly accused men by making immediate communication. Jago is about five feet four inches high. He is spare and wiry; his complexion is extremely pale; his eyes are dark, and very bright and restless. The lower part of his face is concealed by a thick black beard and moustache. The whole appearance of the man is wild and flighty.*

I added the date and the address. That evening a servant was sent on horseback to Narrabee to procure the insertion of the advertisement in the next issue of the newspaper.

When we parted that night, Naomi looked almost like her brighter and happier self. Now that the advertisement was on its way to the printing-office, she was more than sanguine: she was certain of the result.

'You don't know how you have comforted me,' she said, in her frank, warm-hearted way, when we parted for the night. 'All the newspapers will copy it, and we shall hear of John Jago before the week is out.' She turned to go, and came back again to me. 'I will never forgive Silas for writing that confession!' she whispered in my ear. 'If he ever lives under the same roof with Ambrose again, I – well, I believe I wouldn't marry Ambrose if he did! There!'

She left me. Through the wakeful hours of the night my mind dwelt on her last words. That she should contemplate, under any circumstances, even the bare possibility of not marrying Ambrose, was, I am ashamed to say, a direct encouragement to certain hopes which I had already begun to form in secret. The next day's mail brought me a letter on business. My clerk wrote to enquire if there was any chance of my returning to England in time to appear in court at the opening of the next law term. I answered, without hesitation, 'It is still impossible for me to fix the date of my return.' Naomi was in the room while I was writing. How would she have answered, I wonder, if I had told her the truth, and said, 'You are responsible for this letter'?

10

The question of time was now a serious question at Morwick Farm. In six weeks, the court for the trial of criminal cases was to be opened at Narrabee.

During this interval, no new event of any importance occurred.

Many idle letters reached us relating to the advertisement for John Jago; but no positive information was received. Not the slightest trace of the lost man turned up. Not the shadow of a doubt was cast on the assertion of the prosecution that his body had been destroyed in the kiln. Silas Meadowcroft held firmly to the horrible confession that he had made. His brother Ambrose, with equal resolution, asserted his innocence, and reiterated the statement which he had already advanced. At regular periods I accompanied Naomi to visit him in the prison. As the day appointed for the opening of the court approached, he seemed to falter a little in his resolution; his manner became restless; and he grew irritably suspicious about the merest trifles. This change did not necessarily imply the consciousness of guilt: it might merely have indicated natural nervous agitation as the time for the trial drew near. Naomi noticed the alteration in her lover. It greatly increased her anxiety, though it never shook her confidence in Ambrose. Except at mealtimes, I was left, during the period of which I am now writing, almost constantly alone with the charming American girl. Miss Meadowcroft searched the newspapers for tidings of the living John Jago in the privacy of her own room. Mr Meadowcroft would see nobody but his daughter and his doctor, and occasionally one or two old friends. I have since had reason to believe that Naomi, in these days of our intimate association, discovered the true nature of the feelings with which she had inspired me. But she kept her secret. Her manner towards me steadily remained the manner of a sister: she never overstepped by a hair's breadth the safe limits of the character she had assumed.

The sittings of the court began. After hearing the evidence, and examining the confession of Silas Meadowcroft, the grand jury found a true bill against both the prisoners. The day appointed for the trial was the first day in the new week.

I had carefully prepared Naomi's mind for the decision of the grand jury. She bore the new blow bravely.

'If you are not tired of it,' she said, 'come with me to the prison tomorrow. Ambrose will need a little comfort by that time.' She paused, and looked at the day's letters lying on the table. 'Still not a word about John Jago,' she said. 'And all the papers have copied the advertisement. I felt so sure we should hear of him long before this!'

'Do you still feel sure that he is living?' I ventured to ask.

'I am as certain of it as ever,' she replied firmly. 'He is somewhere in hiding: perhaps he is in disguise. Suppose we know no more of him than we know now, when the trial begins? Suppose the jury –' She stopped, shuddering. Death – shameful death on the scaffold – might be the terrible result of the consultation of the jury. 'We have waited for news to come to us long enough,' Naomi resumed. 'We must find the tracks of John Jago for ourselves. There is a week yet before the trial begins. Who will help me to make enquiries? Will you be the man, friend Lefrank?'

It is needless to add (though I knew nothing would come of it) that I consented to be the man.

We arranged to apply that day for the order of admission to the prison, and, having seen Ambrose, to devote ourselves immediately to the contemplated search. How that search was to be conducted was more than I could tell, and more than Naomi could tell. We were to begin by applying to the police to help us to find John Jago, and we were then to be guided by circumstances. Was there ever a more hopeless programme than this?

'Circumstances' declared themselves against us at starting. I applied, as usual, for the order of admission to the prison, and the order was for the first time refused; no reason being assigned by the persons in authority for taking this course. Enquire as I might, the only answer given was, 'Not today.'

At Naomi's suggestion, we went to the prison to seek the explanation which was refused to us at the office. The gaoler on duty at the outer gate was one of Naomi's many admirers. He solved the mystery cautiously in a whisper. The sheriff and the governor of the prison were then speaking privately with Ambrose Meadowcroft in his cell: they had expressly directed that no persons should be admitted to see the prisoner that day but themselves.

What did it mean? We returned, wondering, to the farm. There Naomi, speaking by chance to one of the female servants, made certain discoveries.

Early that morning the sheriff had been brought to Morwick by an old friend of the Meadowcrofts. A long interview had been held between Mr Meadowcroft and his daughter and the official personage introduced by the friend. Leaving the farm, the sheriff had gone straight to the prison, and had proceeded with the governor to visit Ambrose in his cell. Was some potent influence being brought privately to bear on Ambrose? Appearances certainly suggested that enquiry. Supposing the influence to have been really exerted, the next question followed: what was the object in view? We could only wait and see.

Our patience was not severely tried. The event of the next day enlightened us in a very unexpected manner. Before noon, the neighbours brought startling news from the prison to the farm.

Ambrose Meadowcroft had confessed himself to be the murderer of John Jago! He had signed the confession in the presence of the sheriff and the governor on that very day!

I saw the document. It is needless to reproduce it here. In substance, Ambrose confessed what Silas had confessed; claiming, however, to have only struck Jago under intolerable provocation, so as to reduce the nature of his offence against the law from murder to manslaughter. Was the confession really the true statement of what had taken place? Or had the sheriff and governor, acting in the interests of the family name, persuaded Ambrose to try this desperate means of escaping the ignominy of death on the scaffold? The sheriff and the governor preserved impenetrable silence until the pressure put on them judicially at the trial obliged them to speak.

Who was to tell Naomi of this last and saddest of all the calamities which had fallen on her? Knowing how I loved her in secret, I felt an invincible reluctance to be the person who revealed Ambrose Meadowcroft's degradation to his betrothed wife. Had any other member of the family told her what had happened? The lawyer was able to answer me: Miss Meadowcroft had told her.

I was shocked when I heard it. Miss Meadowcroft was the last person in the house to spare the poor girl: Miss Meadowcroft would make the hard tidings doubly terrible to bear in the telling. I tried to find Naomi, without success. She had been always accessible at other times. Was she hiding herself from me now? The idea occurred to me as I was descending the stairs after vainly knocking at the door of her room. I was determined to see her. I waited a few minutes, and then ascended the stairs again suddenly. On the landing I met her, just leaving the room.

She tried to run back. I caught her by the arm, and detained her. With her free hand she held her handkerchief over her face so as to hide it from me.

'You once told me I had comforted you,' I said to her, gently. 'Won't you let me comfort you now?'

She still struggled to get away, and still kept her head turned from me.

'Don't you see that I am ashamed to look you in the face?' she said, in low broken tones. 'Let me go.'

I still persisted in trying to soothe her. I drew back to the window-seat. I said I would wait until she was able to speak to me.

She dropped on the seat, and wrung her hands on her lap. Her downcast eyes still obstinately avoided meeting mine.

'Oh!' she said to herself, 'What madness possessed me? Is it possible that I ever disgraced myself by loving Ambrose Meadowcroft?' She shuddered as the idea found its way to expression on her lips. The tears rolled slowly over her cheeks. 'Don't despise me, Mr Lefrank!' she said, faintly.

I tried, honestly tried, to put the confession before her in its least unfavourable light.

'His resolution has given way,' I said. 'He has done this, despairing of proving his innocence, in terror of the scaffold.'

She rose, with an angry stamp of the foot. She turned her face on me with the deep-red flush of shame in it, and the big tears glistening in her eyes.

'No more of him!' she said, sternly. 'If he is not a murderer, what else is he? A liar and a coward! In which of his characters does he disgrace me most? I have done with him for ever! I will never speak to him again!' She pushed me furiously away from her; advanced a few steps towards her own door; stopped, and came back to me. The generous nature of the girl spoke in her next words. 'I am not ungrateful to *you*, friend Lefrank. A woman in my place is only a woman; and, when she is shamed as I am, she feels it very bitterly. Give me your hand! God bless you!'

She put my hand to her lips before I was aware of her, and kissed it, and ran back to her room.

I sat down at the place which she had occupied. She had

looked at me for one moment when she kissed my hand. I forgot Ambrose and his confession; I forgot the coming trial; I forgot my professional duties and my English friends. There I sat, in a fool's Elysium of my own making, with absolutely nothing in my mind but the picture of Naomi's face at the moment when she had last looked at me!

I have already mentioned that I was in love with her. I merely add this to satisfy you that I tell the truth.

11

Miss Meadowcroft and I were the only representatives of the family at the farm who attended the trial. We went separately to Narrabee. Excepting the ordinary greetings at morning and night, Miss Meadowcroft had not said one word to me since the time when I told her that I did *not* believe John Jago to be a living man.

I have purposely abstained from encumbering my narrative with legal details. I now propose to state the nature of the defence in the briefest outline only.

We insisted on making both prisoners plead 'Not guilty'. This done, we took an objection to the legality of the proceedings at starting. We appealed to the old English law that there should be no conviction for murder until the body of the murdered person was found, or proof of its destruction obtained beyond a doubt. We denied that sufficient proof had been obtained in the case now before the court.

The judges consulted, and decided that the trial should go on. We took our next objection when the confessions were produced in evidence. We declared that they had been extorted by terror, or by undue influence, and we pointed out certain minor peculiarities in which the two confessions failed to corroborate each other. For the rest, our defence on this occasion was, as to essentials, what our defence had been at the enquiry before the magistrate. Once more the judges consulted, and once more they overruled our objection. The confessions were admitted in evidence.

On their side, the prosecution produced one new witness in support of their case. It is needless to waste time in recapitulating his evidence. He contradicted himself gravely on cross-examination. We showed plainly, and after investigation proved, that he was not to be believed on his oath.

The Chief Justice summed up.

He charged, in relation to the confessions, that no weight should be attached to confession incited by hope or fear; and he left it to the jury to determine whether the confessions in this case had been so influenced. In the course of the trial, it had been shown for the defence that the sheriff and the governor had told Ambrose, with his father's knowledge and sanction, that the case was clearly against him; that the only chance of sparing his family the disgrace of his death by public execution lay in making a confession; and that they would do their best, if he did confess, to have his sentence commuted to transportation for life. As for Silas, he was proved to have been beside himself with terror when he made his abominable charge against his brother. We had vainly trusted to the evidence on these two points to induce the court to reject the confessions, and we were destined to be once more disappointed in anticipating that the same evidence would influence the verdict of the jury on the side of mercy. After an absence of an hour, they returned to court with a verdict of 'Guilty' against both the prisoners.

Being asked in due form if they had anything to say in mitigation of their sentence, Ambrose and Silas solemnly declared their innocence, and publicly acknowledged that their respective confessions had been wrung from them with the hope of escaping the hangman's hands. This statement was not noticed by the bench. The prisoners were both sentenced to death.

On my return to the farm, I did not see Naomi. Miss Meadowcroft informed her of the result of the trial. Half an hour later, one of the women servants handed to me an envelope bearing my name on it in Naomi's handwriting.

The envelope enclosed a letter, and with it a slip of paper on which Naomi had hurriedly written these words, 'For God's sake, read this letter I send to you, and do something about it immediately!'

I looked at the letter. It assumed to be written by a gentleman in New York. Only the day before, he had, by the merest accident, seen the advertisement for John Jago, cut out of a newspaper and pasted into a book of 'curiosities' kept by a friend. Upon this he wrote to Morwick Farm to say that he had seen a man exactly answering to the description of John Jago, but bearing another name, working as a clerk in a merchant's office in Jersey City. Having time to spare before the mail went out, he had returned to the office to take another look at the man before he posted his letter. To his surprise he was informed that the clerk had not appeared at his desk that day. His employer had sent to his lodgings, and had been informed that he had suddenly packed up his bag after reading the newspaper at breakfast; had paid his rent honestly, and had gone away, nobody knew where!

It was late in the evening when I read these lines. I had time for reflection before it would be necessary for me to act.

Assuming the letter to be genuine, and adopting Naomi's explanation of the motive which had led John Jago to absent himself secretly from the farm, I reached the conclusion that the search for him might be usefully limited to Narrabee and the surrounding neighbourhood.

The newspaper at his breakfast had no doubt given him his first information of the 'finding' of the grand jury, and of the trial to follow. It was in my experience of human nature that he should venture back to Narrabee in these circumstances, and under the influence of his infatuation for Naomi. More than this, it was again in my experience, I am sorry to say, that he should attempt to make the critical position of Ambrose a means of extorting Naomi's consent to listen favourably to his suit. Cruel indifference to the injury and the suffering which his sudden absence might inflict on others, was plainly implied in his secret withdrawal from the farm. The same cruel indifference, pushed to a further extreme, might well lead him to press his proposals privately on Naomi, and to fix her acceptance of them as the price for saving her cousin's life.

To these conclusions I arrived after much thinking. I had determined, on Naomi's account, to clear the matter up. But it is only candid to add, that my doubts of John Jago's existence remained unshaken by the letter. I believed it to be nothing more or less than a heartless and stupid 'hoax'.

The striking of the hall clock roused me from my meditations. I counted the strokes – midnight!

I rose to go up to my room. Everybody else in the farm had retired to bed, as usual, more than an hour since. The stillness in the house was breathless. I walked softly, by instinct, as I crossed the room to look out at the night. A lovely moonlight met my view: it was like the moonlight on the fatal evening when Naomi had met John Jago on the garden walk.

My bedroom candle was on the side-table: I had just lit it. I was just leaving the room, when the door suddenly opened, and Naomi herself stood before me!

Recovering the first shock of her sudden appearance, I saw instantly, in her eager eyes, in her deadly pale cheeks, that something serious had happened. A large cloak was thrown over her; a white handkerchief was tied over her head. Her hair was in disorder: she had evidently just risen in fear and in haste from her bed.

'What is it?' I asked, advancing to meet her.

She clung trembling with agitation to my arm.

'John Jago!' she whispered.

You will think my obstinacy invincible. I could hardly believe it, even then!

'Do you mean John Jago's ghost?' I asked.

'I have seen John Jago himself,' she answered.

'Where?'

'In the backyard, under my bedroom window!'

The emergency was far too serious to allow of any consideration for the small proprieties of everyday life.

'Let *me* see him!' I said.

'I am here to fetch you,' she replied, in her frank and fearless way. 'Come upstairs with me.' Her room was on the first floor of the house, and was the only bedroom which looked out on the backyard. On our way up the stairs, she told me what had happened.

'I was in bed,' she said, 'but not asleep, when I heard a pebble strike against the window-pane. I waited, wondering what it meant. Another pebble was thrown against the glass. So far I was surprised, but not frightened. I got up, and ran to the window to look out. There was John Jago, looking up at me in the moonlight!'

'Did he see you?'

'Yes. He said, "Come down and speak to me! I have something serious to say to you!"'

'Did you answer him?'

'As soon as I could fetch my breath, I said, "Wait a little," and ran downstairs to you. What shall I do?'

'Let *me* see him, and I will tell you.'

We entered her room. Keeping cautiously behind the window-curtain, I looked out.

There he was! His beard and moustache were shaved off: his hair was cut close. But there was no disguising his wild brown eyes, or the peculiar movement of his spare wiry figure, as he walked slowly to and fro in the moonlight, waiting for Naomi. For the moment, my own agitation almost over-powered me: I had so firmly disbelieved that John Jago was a living man!

'What shall I do?' Naomi repeated.

'Is the door to the dairy open?' I asked.

'No; but the door of the tool-house, round the corner, is not locked.'

'Very good. Show yourself at the window, and say to him, "I am coming directly".'

The brave girl obeyed me without a moment's hesitation.

There had been no doubt about his eyes and his gait; there was no doubt now about his voice as he answered softly from below, 'All right!'

'Keep him talking to you where he is now,' I said to Naomi, 'until I have time to get round by the other way to the tool-house. Then pretend to be fearful of discovery at the dairy; and bring him round the corner, so that I can hear him behind the door.'

We left the house together, and separated silently. Naomi followed my instructions with a woman's quick intelligence where stratagems are concerned. I had hardly been a minute in the tool-house before I heard him speaking to Naomi on the other side of the door.

The first words which I caught distinctly related to his motive for secretly leaving the farm. Mortified pride – doubly mortified by Naomi's contemptuous refusal, and by the personal indignity offered to him by Ambrose – was at the bottom of his conduct in absenting himself from Morwick. He owned that he had seen the advertisement, and that it had actually encouraged him to keep in hiding!

'After being laughed at and insulted and denied, I was glad,' said the miserable wretch, 'to see that some of you had serious reason to wish me back again. It rests with you, Miss Naomi, to keep me here, and to persuade me to save Ambrose by showing myself, and owning my name.'

'What do you mean?' I heard Naomi ask, sternly.

He lowered his voice; but I could still hear him.

'Promise you will marry me,' he said, 'and I will go before the magistrate tomorrow, and show him that I am a living man.'

'Suppose I refuse?'

'In that case you will lose me again, and none of you will find me till Ambrose is hanged.'

'Are you villain enough, John Jago, to mean what you say?' asked the girl, raising her voice.

'If you attempt to give the alarm,' he answered, 'as true as God above us, you will feel my hand on your throat! It's my turn now, miss; and I am not to be trifled with. Will you have me for your husband – yes or no?'

'No!' she answered, loudly and firmly.

I threw open the door, and seized him as he lifted his hand on her. He had not suffered from the nervous derangement which had weakened me, and he was the stronger man of the two. Naomi saved my life. She struck up his pistol as he pulled it out of his pocket with his free hand and presented it at my head. The bullet was fired into the air. I tripped his heels at the same moment. The report of the pistol had alarmed the house. We two together kept him on the ground until help arrived.

12

John Jago was brought before the magistrate, and John Jago was identified the next day.

The lives of Ambrose and Silas were, of course, no longer in peril, so far as human justice was concerned. But there were legal delays to be encountered, and legal formalities to be observed, before the brothers could be released from prison in the characters of innocent men.

During the interval which thus elapsed, certain events happened which may be briefly mentioned here before I close my narrative.

Mr Meadowcroft the elder, broken by the suffering which he had gone through, died suddenly of a rheumatic affection of the heart. A codicil attached to his will abundantly justified what Naomi had told me of Miss Meadowcroft's influence over her father, and of the end she had in view in exercising it. A life-income only was left to Mr Meadowcroft's sons. The freehold of the farm was bequeathed to his daughter, with the testator's recommendation added that she should marry his 'best and dearest friend, Mr John Jago'.

Armed with the power of the will, the heiress of Morwick sent an insolent message to Naomi requesting her no longer to consider herself one of the inmates of the farm. Miss Meadowcroft, it should be here added, positively refused to believe that John Jago had ever asked Naomi to be his wife, or had ever threatened her, as I had heard him threaten her, if she refused. She accused me, as she accused Naomi, of trying meanly to injure John Jago in her estimation, out of hatred towards 'that much injured man'. And she sent to me, as she sent to Naomi, a formal notice to leave the house.

We two banished ones met the same day in the hall, with our travelling bags in our hands.

'We are turned out together, friend Lefrank,' said Naomi, with her quaintly comical smile. 'You will go back to England, I guess; and I must make my own living in my own country. Women can get employment in the States if they have a friend to speak for them. Where shall I find somebody who can give me a place?'

I saw my way to saying the right word at the right moment.

'I have got a place to offer you,' I replied, 'if you see no objection to accepting it.'

She suspected nothing, so far.

'That's lucky, sir,' was all she said. 'Is it in a telegraph-office or in a dry-goods store?'

I astonished my little American friend by taking her then and there in my arms, and giving her my first kiss.

'The office is by my fireside,' I said. 'The salary is anything in reason you like to ask me for. And the place, Naomi, if you have no objection to it, is the place of my wife.'

I have no more to say, except that years have passed since I spoke those words, and that I am as fond of Naomi as ever.

Some months after our marriage, Mrs Lefrank wrote to a friend at Narrabee for news of what was going on at the farm. The answer informed us that Ambrose and Silas had emigrated to New Zealand, and that Miss Meadowcroft was alone at Morwick Farm. John Jago had refused to marry her. John Jago had disappeared again, nobody knew where.

AUTHOR'S NOTE

The first idea of this little story was suggested to the author by a printed account of a trial which took place, early in the present century, in the United States. The recently published narrative of the case is entitled 'The Trial, Confessions and Conviction of Jesse and Stephen Boorn for the murder of Russell Colvin, and the return of the man supposed to have been murdered. By Hon. Leonard Sergeant, Ex-Lieutenant-Governor of Vermont. (Manchester, Vermont, *Journal Book and Job Office*, 1873).' It may not be amiss to add, for the benefit of incredulous readers, that all the 'improbable events' in the story are matters of fact, taken from the printed narrative. Anything which 'looks like truth' is, in nine cases out of ten, the invention of the author.

$- W. C.$

BIOGRAPHICAL NOTE

William Wilkie Collins, author of the first detective novels in English, was born in 1824. The son of a respected landscape painter, he was named after his painter godfather, David Wilkie. Educated in London, Collins studied to become a barrister, although it was never his intention to practise, and by 1848 he had turned to writing, a number of short works appearing in Charles Dickens' periodicals, *Household Words* and later, *All the Year Round*. A first novel, *Iolani*, set in ancient Tahiti and involving sorcery and sacrifice, though perhaps written as early as 1844, was later rejected by publishers (and only rediscovered and published for the first time in 1999). Collins' first venture into crime fiction was *Basil* (1852), a Gothic tale of doppelgangers, bigamy, and hidden family secrets. Developing at once detective fiction and the novel of sensation, Collins' exotic and gripping stories – often involving strong heroines, sinister locales, charlatans, and physical or psychological afflictions – became hugely popular with the reading public. His great novels appeared in the 1860s, when, at the height of his powers, Collins' wrote *The Woman in White* (1860), *No Name* (1862), *Armadale* (1866), and *The Moonstone* (1868).

Unafraid to question Victorian social mores, Collins never married but maintained two families. He lived both with Caroline Graves (whom he met in a midnight encounter similar to that in *The Woman in White*) and Martha Rudd. In later life, Collins became addicted to opium, and the novels he wrote between 1870 and 1889 – concerned with social issues – are considered inferior to his earlier output. Recently, however, Collins' oeuvre has received renewed critical attention, a recent biography hailing him as the king of inventors.

HESPERUS PRESS – 100 PAGES

Hesperus Press, as suggested by the Latin motto, is committed to bringing near what is far – far both in space and time. Works written by the greatest authors, and unjustly neglected or simply little known in the English-speaking world, are made accessible through new translations and a completely fresh editorial approach. Through these short classic works, each little more than 100 pages in length, the reader will be introduced to the greatest writers from all times and all cultures.

For more information on Hesperus Press, please visit our website: **www.hesperuspress.com**

To place an order, please contact:
Grantham Book Services
Isaac Newton Way
Alma Park Industrial Estate
Grantham
Lincolnshire NG31 9SD
Tel: +44 (0) 1476 541080
Fax: +44 (0) 1476 541061
Email: orders@gbs.tbs-ltd.co.uk

SELECTED TITLES FROM HESPERUS PRESS

Gustave Flaubert *Memoirs of a Madman*

Alexander Pope *Scriblerus*

Ugo Foscolo *Last Letters of Jacopo Ortis*

Anton Chekhov *The Story of a Nobody*

Joseph von Eichendorff *Life of a Good-for-nothing*

Mark Twain *The Diary of Adam and Eve*

Giovanni Boccaccio *Life of Dante*

Victor Hugo *The Last Day of a Condemned Man*

Joseph Conrad *Heart of Darkness*

Edgar Allan Poe *Eureka*

Emile Zola *For a Night of Love*

Daniel Defoe *The King of Pirates*

Giacomo Leopardi *Thoughts*

Nikolai Gogol *The Squabble*

Franz Kafka *Metamorphosis*

Herman Melville *The Enchanted Isles*

Leonardo da Vinci *Prophecies*

Charles Baudelaire *On Wine and Hashish*

William Makepeace Thackeray *Rebecca and Rowena*

Théophile Gautier *The Jinx*

Charles Dickens *The Haunted House*

Luigi Pirandello *Loveless Love*

Fyodor Dostoevsky *Poor People*

E.T.A. Hoffmann *Mademoiselle de Scudéri*

Henry James *In the Cage*

Francesco Petrarch *My Secret Book*

André Gide *Theseus*

D.H. Lawrence *The Fox*

Percy Bysshe Shelley *Zastrozzi*